The Midnight Saint

Mitchel Whitington

ISBN 978-1-9393060-9-8

Library of Congress Control Number: 2014942319

© 2014 Mitchel Whitington
All Rights Reserved

Printed in the United States of America
Published by 23 House Publishing
SAN 299-8084
www.23house.com

For Amy

Table of Contents

The First Day

Wednesday, December 13th

"How far?"

"About a hundred-thirty miles, or seventeen gallons of gas, based on the last tank," she said, staring at the map and mentally adding the numbers between the state line and Little Rock. "Wait, we're still thirty miles from the state line so add another couple of gallons."

"Crap," Daniel sighed under his breath, closing his eyes and resting his face in his hands. "We're in some real trouble here, Jen."

"How much do we have?" she asked cautiously.

"Fifteen bucks and change. Nowhere near enough for the gas."

The old brown sedan had coasted into the station on fumes. The paint was fading, and peeling on top, and the automobile that was so grand in its day was holding on for dear life. Despite the bald tires, the torn upholstery and the sagging headliner, a rosary and cross hanging from the rear-view mirror lent a ray of hope to the car. In the back seat, a child stirred.

1

"Mom? Dad? Are we there yet?"

"No honey; go back to sleep. We're still a few hours away," Jen said, desperately trying to comfort her daughter. She watched as the girl laid her head back down in the seat, foggy from a child's slumber.

Daniel sighed. "Geez, four years old already, and this is all we can give her." He felt the weight of the world pressing down on him in the front seat of the car.

"We'll be fine. The job's waiting. All we have to do is get to Little Rock."

He shook his head in frustration. "I know, Jen, but how in the world are we going to do that? We're out of money, and almost out of time. It was unbelievably great of your sister to get me this job. If I don't show up by tomorrow morning, though, not only will I lose the gig, but I'll never be able to face your family again."

"C'mon Daniel, everyone knows that it wasn't your fault that the garage closed down. You were the best mechanic in the place, and you always had people asking for you personally to work on their car," she said, smiling at her husband, genuinely proud. She reached over and gently pushed a tuft of hair off his forehead. "So a mom and pop shop couldn't keep up with the national chains. We'll survive. We'll stay with Suzi and Jim for a month, bank a couple of checks, and then find a place of our own."

"I know, I know. I just wish that we hadn't drained our savings in the mean time. So now we're in the middle of nowhere, out of money, out of gas, and a couple of hours away from our last chance. Any ideas?"

"Shhh. Mandy's asleep," she whispered. "Don't talk about M-O-N-E-Y and get her upset."

"I'm upset about M-O-N-E-Y!" Daniel said. "But we've got to hit Little Rock tonight." He looked around the gas station, and then opened the door of the car. "Stay here. I'll see what I can do." Daniel took a deep breath, and then climbed out into the cold night air.

Jen glanced over the seat to check on her daughter, then closed her eyes tightly and prayed hard for their delivery. Opening her eyes, she looked through the windshield and saw the desperation on her husband's face as he stood helplessly at the front of the car. She thought of the day, December thirteenth, and then closed her eyes once again. Whispering the words from her youth, she began to softly say, "Saint Lucia, virgin and martyr, hear my prayer and obtain my petition..."

* * * * *

It had honestly been a good day. With the ups and downs of the economy, Adam's career had been a roller coaster ride over the last year. Today, however, they had received the final word on the lumber factory where half of the town worked: it would remain open, at least for the foreseeable future. There had been an understandable celebration all afternoon, and everyone drifted out early for the day to rush home and tell the good news to their families. Adam had done just the opposite, calling his wife on the phone, and then staying to take advantage of the quiet time to finish up some of the work that had been piling up on his desk. With the possibility of the factory closing looming over their heads, work had slowed to a snail's pace as people worried more and more. It was especially true in supplies and procurement, the department that Adam headed. His group had the responsibility for acquiring every item that rolled through the gates of the plant, from bread for the cafeteria to the timber that would be turned into plywood, planking, and other lumber products – none of which seemed to matter if the place was shut down. Christmas was also less than two weeks away and the end of the year was around the corner. Even with the good news that had just been received, the work at the plant would soon be grinding to a halt for the holidays.

Adam started out as a clerk in the department the summer after he graduated from high school, and had shown a genuine talent for working with the numbers and juggling the orders and schedules generated by the group. Every few years he had been given more responsibility, slowly rising through the organizational chart. Two years ago, his boss and friend had called him into his office, closed the door, and told him that he was retiring. His choice for replacement was Adam. The new position brought longer hours and more work, and while he didn't exactly have a passion for his job, he was good at it and loved working with the people in the department. In the past few months, however, Adam had spent many a night tossing and turning in bed, wondering where they would all find jobs if the plant did indeed close.

Fortunately, that was no longer a worry. Hopefully the wheels of the lumber plant would continue to turn. He had at least done his part, completing the sizable stack of work on his desk before locking up his office and walking through the dusk to his pickup. Leaving work this late afforded him the luxury of a leisurely drive home, away from any rush-hour traffic. Christmas decorations were just starting to be turned on as darkness fell, filling Adam with the warmth and nostalgia of the season. There had been a blanketing snowfall earlier in the week, with an occasional flurry here and there since, leaving patchy areas of white in small drifts beside the road. Most yards had a light covering of snow, setting off the brilliantly colored decorations. The Christmas season was Adam's favorite time of the year.

As he drove, he noticed that the truck had dropped below the halfway mark on the gas gauge. Adam considered waiting, but knew that it would be one less thing to remember to do. Putting on his blinker, he turned in to the convenience store by the main highway and wheeled up to one of the gas pumps. He opened the door of his pickup, and stepped into the brisk night air.

Like thousands of other times, he mechanically removed the gas cap, lifted the nozzle, inserted it and squeezed the trigger to begin pumping. Nothing happened. Adam shook his head, removed his wallet, and then went through the credit card pay-at-the-pump procedure. He heard a mechanical click inside the pump, so he squeezed the trigger again and the gasoline began to flow. With one last adjustment he set the handle for automatic cut-off, and then leaned back against the truck to wait.

The monotony was broken by a young man, perhaps twenty-five, who lumbered cautiously over to him from a rough-looking car in the other pump lane. He looked lean and a bit haggard, but for a reason that he couldn't explain Adam sensed that there was something good about him.

"Evening, Mister," the young man said. "How are you doing?"

"Oh, 'bout right," Adam replied casually. The question had obviously been rhetorical, so he just stood there listening to the gas pump churning the liquid into the truck, waiting to hear what was really on the young man's mind.

"You interested in buying some tools?" the fellow asked hopefully. "I've got a great wrench set that cost me a couple hundred bucks a year or so ago. I'll let you have it for forty."

Adam stared at him, trying to size up what was behind the offer.

"They're not stolen or anything, Mister. They're mine. I'm a mechanic, and most guys in my job are expected to have their own tools."

Adam was suspicious. "So why sell them?" he asked. "Getting out of the business?"

5

"No, I don't want to sell them. Not really. But I have a job waiting for me in Little Rock tomorrow and..." his voice softened; he looked down. "We don't have the money to get there. We're going to stay with my sister-in-law, and I can probably borrow somebody's tools until I can buy my own again, but I have to get there for work in the morning. Please, Mister, the tools are good, and worth a whole lot more."

Adam hesitated, and then reached in his back pocket for his wallet. "Go get'em," he said. Taking out a twenty and two tens, he heard the nozzle snap off indicating that his truck was full of gas. As he returned the nozzle and pulled the receipt from the slot on the pump, he could hear the young man rummaging in the trunk of the car. The fellow emerged with a bright red, metal box, almost the size of a briefcase, and slammed the lid of the trunk shut.

As he walked over to the truck, Adam said, "Let's see'em." The young man opened the case, revealing rows of chrome wrenches, drivers and tools of every shape and size. The overhead florescent lights played on the brilliant metal. Adam admired how neatly they were arranged, and even though they showed signs of wear, it was obvious that they were well cared for, the way that any fine craftsman would do with the tools of his trade. Adam nodded his head, satisfied with what he saw, and smiled at the man. "Here you go," he said, extending the forty dollars and accepting the open case. He rested it across the corner of the truck's bed.

"I can't thank you enough," the young man said. "You got a heck of a deal on the tools, but more than that, you'll never know how much you've helped us out tonight. I really do appreciate it." He walked around to the car as he talked.

"No problem. Just do well at the new job. Oh, and you're going to have to go in and pay before pumping," Adam said. He smiled at the man, and nodded toward the convenience store.

"Oh, right; thanks. And thanks again for helping us out," the young man said, and started walking away with a glint of hope in his eyes.

Adam sighed, and looked once again at the tools. He took his wallet back out, removed another twenty, and laid it on top of the shining wrenches. Snapping the case shut, he glanced back over his shoulder to make sure that he wasn't seen.

* * * * *

Jen sat in silence. She had heard Daniel removing the tools that were so precious to him from the trunk. She watched in the mirror as he sold them to a stranger, an act that had to have been incredibly painful. But inside, she marveled at his strength. He had to really believe in this chance. She knew at that very moment that they were going to be just fine. Once again, she closed her eyes tightly. As she softly whispered "Thank you," under her breath, there was a knock on the window of the car.

Standing beside her door was the man who bought the tools, gesturing toward her with the case. She rolled down her window, and he handed it inside.

"Your fellow seems like a proud man, and I expect that you folks are at your last straw for him to sell something so precious just to get gas money."

"We are," she said softly.

"Well, far be it from me to interfere with your plans. Take back the tools. It sounds like you two have a great opportunity. Go make it work," he said, winked, and walked away.

As the pickup truck pulled onto the city street and sped away, Daniel opened the door of the car and looked inside. "Everything okay?" he asked.

Jen sat crying. "Look, Daniel, just take a look at this. That fellow gave your tools back, and–"

7

Daniel saw the twenty laying in the open case, and shook his head. "Man." He stood up, looking after the pickup. "Thanks," he called in the general direction that the stranger had gone, knowing there was no way that he would ever be able to express the full measure of his appreciation.

He stuck his head back into the car. "Wake Mandy up and see if she'd like a soda," he said, smiling. I'm going to fill up the car with gas, so why don't you walk over to the pay phone and tell Suzi and Jim that we'll be there soon." He stopped to look into his wife's eyes. "This is going to happen, Jen. This is all going to work out."

She nodded her head, and looked at him through a teary haze. "I know it will, Daniel, I know it will."

* * * * *

Adam had driven out of the lights of the small town and into the rural countryside where he lived. The moonlight shown on the fields, reflecting off the snow, a white blanket broken only by the occasional barren elm or oak. A sharp contrast to the Christmas lights a few miles behind him, the serene landscape was breathtaking in its simplicity. He was only a mile from home now, passing familiar landmarks that he had known from his youth. Fennway's barn on the right, perpetually in need of a coat of paint, the Community church on the left a hundred yards further up, and finally the pond in Darden's pasture where he and his friends had swam and fished every summer of their boyhood.

Tonight, the pond shined like a mirror, reflecting the thousands of stars overhead. As he passed it, Adam caught something out of the corner of his eye. A young girl, seventeen or eighteen years old at the most, was seemingly skating across the white field toward the pond. He slowed down, knowing full well that the pond had never frozen over. Still, she skimmed

8

right onto it, and across the water as if she was an Olympic skater with the grace of a ballerina. She wore a flowing white gown, had long black hair, and her face shown as if it was illuminated by a halo of light.

Adam was both captivated and mystified by her. Just as he had convinced himself that it was some dream or illusion, she turned her head toward him. The distance did not seem to matter. They might have been only a few feet apart. Her eyes were gleaming, deep, and seemed to look into his very soul. For a moment, he was lost – a thousand miles away, not knowing or caring about anything else, but then she turned suddenly away, and glided away into the distance.

Adam shook his head, marveling at the incident. "Whew!" he sighed aloud. "I've got to stop working so late." As he pondered the sight, he slowed the truck and turned into the long gravel driveway toward his home.

* * * * *

Adam opened his eyes, looking around the dark bedroom to get his bearings. After a moment for his eyes to focus, he was able to see the digital clock on the dresser. It read 12:00 AM. The initial moments of disorientation passed – the time when fantasy bleeds into the real world. He had been dreaming, seeing the girl again, wondering who she was. He seemed to be traveling with her as she moved faster and faster across the countryside, their feet barely brushing the ground. He felt the cold December air in his face, and the halo of light around her head drew him closer. In the distance he had heard a dog barking, and as it got louder his conscious mind took control and woke him. It was their basset hound, Elvis, and he was sensing something out of the ordinary.

Elvis had innumerable barks, howls, grunts and whines, all meaning something in a basset language that he just couldn't seem to make humans understand. Adam recognized this particular bark, though, as one that Elvis used when something odd was going on. He glanced over to make sure that Emily was okay, and saw that she was still sleeping soundly. Hopefully, he'd be able to quiet Elvis before he disturbed her.

Emily was truly the love of his life. They had started dating while still in high school, married when they graduated and attended junior college while they both held down jobs. Her long, flowing red hair had initially caught his attention, with her deep green eyes accenting a naturally beautiful, always smiling face. He leaned over and gently kissed her cheek, then carefully got out of bed and felt around the room for his blue jeans. Adam pulled them on, slipped on an old pair of sneakers that had been demoted to house shoes, and crept out of the room.

Even though Elvis was a fifty-pound basset, he was a house dog. Adam often joked with people that no one had ever told Elvis that he wasn't a lap dog, either, since visitors could judge how well they met with the dog's approval by the amount of time it took him to jump up into their lap, lick their face, then nuzzle in for a nap. Elvis had a doggie-door from the kitchen to the back yard, which was enclosed by a chain-link fence. Elvis was in the yard tonight, baying at some situation that he obviously didn't think was quite right.

Adam had reached the back door and opened it, already trying to find out what was going on. "Elvis?" he called in a soft voice. "C'mon boy!" As he stepped through the door and onto the back patio, he was immediately bathed in brilliant, white light. His body seized, temporarily in shock.

Adam didn't know how long he stood there, or at what point Elvis stopped barking. His eyes were transfixed on the center of the yard, where the young girl that he had seen earlier stood – or rather hovered – a few inches off the ground. Her white robes illuminated the entire yard, and around the top of her head shown a halo of light that could only be described as pure. It was a light such as Adam had never seen, and he knew that he was in the presence of something mystical.

"W-who are you?" he stammered, unable to mask the awe in his voice.

The girl smiled, nodded her head once, and simply said, "I am Lucia."

A thousand thoughts raced through Adam's mind. What to say, how to begin, and other innumerable questions formed in his mind, but he opened his mouth and could only say again, "Who are you?"

Again, the girl replied "Lucia." She took several steps toward him, her feet now lightly brushing the ground. A few yards from Adam, she stopped.

"What do you want?" he finally asked with an unwavering gaze.

"Be calm, Adam, you do not have anything to fear. I am here to tell you something. And to give you something."

"Okay… but, I don't understand…" he said.

She smiled again. "Tonight you helped a couple with a small child. They were in desperate need. Very important people, as it will turn out; especially the daughter. The mother asked for my intercession on her behalf, which I gladly gave. The help that you were supposed to supply was to purchase the man's tools to give them the money that they needed to carry on. But you did much more." Her hands had been clasped in front of her, but she now opened them toward Adam. "So here I am. I have something to tell you, and something to give you. Take my hands."

He apprehensively reached out, and as his hands touched Lucia's he felt his body charge with electricity. He felt warm in the midst of the cold winter air, safe in the presence of this being. He was not afraid. He stepped back, rubbing his hands together, and said, "I'm sorry. It's just that you're so, well,

11

different from what I'm used to seeing in my back yard. This is going to sound crazy, and I can't believe that I'm asking it, but are you an angel?" he asked cautiously.

"I am not an angel," she said with a soft, sweet voice. "Angels are busy on other matters. Some would call me Saint Lucia, but you do not have to be so formal. I am simply Lucia."

"A ghost then?" He studied her as he waited for her reply.

"Nor a ghost. At least... not in the sense to which you refer." She stooped down, and then sat on the ground. Elvis was on her, looking for attention before she settled. He stood with his front paws in her lap, completely calm as she gently stroked his back. "I love animals so much," she said, laughing at his sad eyes and drooping basset face. "But back to your question. I am not some disembodied spirit, wandering the Earth – which is what I assume you describe. I guess that the easiest way to explain it is that I was once a living human, just like yourself, but a very long time ago. I died, but I have come to you at God's instruction tonight to deliver a message on his behalf."

"God?" Adam asked, his eyebrows rising. "God like in the Community Church up the road? Like in Sunday School? *GOD* God?"

"God that lives in your heart, Adam," she replied evenly, her eyes staring up into Adam's as she continued to stroke the dog.

"I'm afraid that you have the wrong guy, Ms. Lucia. I'm certainly not the kind of guy that a saint would be visiting, because I haven't been to church in..."

"That is not how you judge people, Adam, and it is certainly not how God does," she interrupted. "He knows you, and He knows your heart. You are a good man, and God is pleased with you."

Adam was silent for a few moments to digest her words. He finally said, "So you're telling me that you actually talk to God?"

She gave Elvis a final pat, and then stood to face Adam. Lucia looked him squarely in the eyes. Her features were delicate, like a young girl who was just becoming a woman. She said, "Only moments before you drove away from the gasoline station, while you were still thinking about your day at work, while your daughter was asleep at your home and dreaming of Christmas morning, I was standing in the very presence of God, just as I now stand in front of you. He told me what I was to do concerning you, what I was to tell you and the gift that I was to give you this midnight." She smiled. "Yes, Adam, I actually talk to God. But I cannot tarry long tonight, so allow me to do His bidding. I am going to give you a lot to think about. I will tell you what He has instructed me to. I have something to share with you... although I fear that it might be difficult for you to hear."

Adam paused, waiting for her to continue, and finally asked, "Yes?"

She sighed. "What I have come to tell you is this: I am afraid that you, Adam, are going to die."

"Die?" Her words had cut through him, and he was caught completely off guard. Adam felt his heart suddenly race. "W-when? How?" he asked. "You can't just throw something like that out there and–"

She raised her hand to stop his questions. "That is all that I am to say about the matter tonight. Except, of course, that you should not be afraid. What will happen will happen, and there is nothing that you can do to evade it."

"But... no..." He looked down for a moment, trying to grasp what she had said. He glanced back up at her. "If God knows me so well, how can he have told you to say that? He must know that there is nothing that terrifies me more than

13

death. Look at me!" he said in a trembling voice. He held out his hands, which were visibly shaking. "I always knew that I would die someday. But to be told that it's about to happen – and what about my family? They need me..." he trailed off, tears welling in his eyes.

"I know that you are afraid, but your fear is of the unknown. Remember that I told you that I had a gift for you as well," she continued, "and it is this: over the next eleven days, I will appear to you every evening, and you may ask me one question about death each night. To help you... prepare. The only condition is that you may ask about the exact nature of your own death only on the last night. Other than that, I will answer questions to help you understand and allay your fears about what is to come. She shrugged her shoulders, and said, "You might say that I am here to counsel you in the matter."

He glanced around the dark patio, mind racing. "But that's not fair – I'm not that old! How can I possibly..."

"Adam," Lucia said calmly, "children die every day. Infants, even. You have lived a full life. How is this unfair?"

"Because I have a daughter – and my wife can't raise her alone, it's too much to ask. They need me!" His tone was desperate, his voice louder.

"And you will wake that family if you raise your voice. We have eleven more nights to discuss the matter. It is not a time to panic."

He took a step back. "Not panic? Not panic, Lucia? What, are you kidding me?" Adam stopped and took a deep breath. "Wait – you said that God sent you. God can do anything, right? He can fix this. If He sent you here, He certainly must not want to see me die."

"God does not want to see anything happen to hurt any of His children. And He has the power to do anything that He wishes – after all, He spoke this entire universe into being. But He also gave man the gift of free will, and so there are things that, even though they might break His heart, He must simply allow to happen." She paused for a moment, looking peacefully at Adam. "And one of those things is your death. I am sure that it will happen, so please accept your gift, which is to allow me to help you prepare."

He quickly did the math in his head. "Okay, but wait – from what you've said, I'm at least going to live until Christmas Day?" he asked hopefully.

Lucia paused, then slowly turned and with a graceful motion started moving away. She moved faster, skating slowly and deliberately across the snow-covered ground. She passed through the chain-link fence surrounding the yard as if it was not there, and as she did she looked back over her shoulder at Adam. "Yes," she said, and disappeared into the night. Elvis ran to the edge of the yard, staring through the fence after her. He whined once, then turned and walked back toward the house, yawning.

Adam sat heavily to the ground and softly said, "Eleven more days; that's almost two weeks. It's plenty of time to figure something out." After a moment of staring into the darkness, he began to sob. "Something…" he said through the tears.

The Second Day

Thursday, December 14th

"What in the world?" Emily said groggily, tying her housecoat. In the kitchen stood Adam, dressed in jeans and a tee shirt, busily scrambling eggs. The aroma of bacon and toasted bread radiated throughout the house.

"Morning, babe!" he said, looking around and flashing a smile that was a little more forced than he would have liked.

She cautiously walked to the bar in the center of the kitchen, and peeked under a paper towel to examine the crisp strips of bacon. "Okay, what gives? You're usually halfway through a bowl of cereal by now. Instead you're cooking a full breakfast?" She narrowed her eyes and shot a suspicious look. "I'm missing something... let me guess. You're already buttering me up to have a Super Bowl party here at the house."

"Not even close. Besides, we had the party this year. It's Tommy's turn for the next one."

"Hmmmm." she said, eyeing him carefully as she walked across the kitchen. "Okay, you've found something that you want for Christmas that's outside of the budget."

"Nope," Adam replied. Two slices of toast popped up from the toaster. He added them to a small stack on a plate, and then started two more.

"Okay, it's something even more devious." She thought for a moment, then slowly shook a finger toward him. "If you have to work on Christmas Day, I'm going to really be..."

"Quite the opposite, actually," he interrupted. "In fact, I'm taking the next two weeks off."

"You're what?" Emily exclaimed, genuinely surprised. "When did this happen?"

"Last night. Well, this morning I guess. Help me set the table and I'll tell you all about it." Adam picked up the spatula, gave the eggs a final stir in the skillet, and then dumped then into a waiting bowl. He tried to be nonchalant and care-free, just as he'd been rehearsing in his mind all night.

Emily was staring at her husband questioningly, but stepped up to the counter, opened a cabinet door and removed three plates. "I think I'd like to hear about this before Amy gets in here. She's brushing her teeth right now, so will you please tell me what's going on?"

"Nothing is going on. I just woke up this morning and started thinking about all the work that I did last night. I got caught up on all the reports that are due this year, finished some general paperwork around the office and even got started on some things that we don't have to work on 'til January. When I was thinking about all that, I realized that it was going to be pretty slow for the next week or so. And you know as well as I do that things at the plant pretty much shut down around Christmas anyway. So I've already phoned my boss and a few of the folks from the office, called in some favors for the few things that I have left to do, and told them that I'd see them after Christmas."

"Kind of sudden, isn't it?" she said, her green eyes studying Adam for any clue as to what was behind the change of direction. She knew her husband as well as she knew herself, and there was something a little off-center this morning. Something wasn't right; something that he wasn't telling her. They never kept secrets from each other. Love and trust were the cornerstones of their marriage. Yet deep inside her gut, Emily knew that something was wrong… and it scared her to death.

"Honey, you're going to have to trust me. So I'll miss a few office parties. I'll get to help out more with the Christmas shopping and I can spend more time with you and Amy," he said, continuing to shuttle the preparations for breakfast between the kitchen countertop and the table.

"Something's wrong, Adam. You're trying to sell me on this idea." Emily had stopped beside the table, and stood in her housecoat with her arms crossed, following her husband with her eyes.

"What could possibly be wrong with wanting to spend more time with my wife and daughter during the holidays?"

She sighed, shaking her head. "Gee, Adam, where do I start? You're taking off two weeks without even consulting me, and you know as well as I do that we talk about everything. You're burning two weeks of vacation that we could be using for a family trip. But more than that, there's something about this that I just don't like. It's spontaneous, and Adam, you don't have a spontaneous bone in your body."

Adam raised a finger and exclaimed "Ah-ha! That may very well be right, because you've been complaining about that since we started dating in high school. Maybe I'm finally trying to make a change in my life to please you."

"I'm pretty comfortable with the way that you are now" she said flatly, unamused. "Adam, there's no way that I can take off from the store. Dad pretty much just shows up to get to visit with his friends who come in. I run the place now. If you do take off all this time, I won't be able to spend it with you. And Amy's in school until the twenty-third."

He sighed. Emily knew that he was hiding something; he could hear it in her voice. And he actually was – one of two things, actually. On one hand, he might be losing his mind, and if that was the case, there's no question that the time off would help him get back on track. On the other hand, if a messenger from God had truly appeared last night, he had even bigger problems. If what the girl had said last night was true, then as unthinkable as it was, he was about to die. Even though waves of nausea came over him with that thought, he knew that he had to put the welfare of Emily and Amy first. With a free schedule during the day, he would be able to take care of all the things that had been running through his mind since his encounter with the girl named Lucia. He didn't know exactly when he was going to die, but since it was apparently eminent – assuming that he really wasn't crazy – he could get everything in order for his wife and daughter. Lucia had said that he would at least be alive through Christmas Eve, so there was no way that he was going to spend what could be the last two weeks of his life at the plant. Besides, with the time off, he hoped to find some way out of the situation – there had to be a possibility of reprieve.

"Yes, but while I'm out running errands and such I'll be able to drop in and see you at the store. We can even have lunch together," he said, trying to win her over.

"You know that most of my lunches are a sandwich from the deli aisle of the store and a soda from the cooler." Emily was still unconvinced. Christmas, like most holidays, was a busy time at the grocery store that had been in her family for three generations. Her grandfather had opened a small market when the town was little more than a few houses clustered around a state highway. When the plant had come in, the population swelled into the hundreds, and finally over a thousand. By the time that her father had taken over the business, it was time to build a larger store to accommodate the town's growth. After she and Adam were married, her father had built an even larger store. It could not compete with the huge national chains, but it served the needs of the community well. In the last five years, her role had changed from that of an administrator to being the full-blown manager. With the holidays ahead, that meant dealing with every crisis from running out of turkeys to employees taking off at the last minute. She shook her head, and said, "I don't know, Adam. Do what you want to do, but I can't shake the feeling that there's something wrong."

Just as she finished speaking, Amy bounded into the room. Eight years old and in the third grade, she was a beautiful child with her mother's flowing red hair. "Wow, who cooked breakfast?" she asked with sparkling eyes.

"I did, sweetheart, just especially for you and your mother." He put the last fork down in its place on the table, and stepped over to his daughter. In one smooth motion, he picked her up and hugged her tightly.

"Hey, I just fixed my hair! Mom, help!" she exclaimed in a fit of giggling.

Emily smiled; maybe nothing was wrong. Maybe this really would be good for Adam. She only knew that she trusted him no matter what, and that if there was something bothering him, he'd tell her in his own time. "C'mon you two, we still have a schedule to keep. Let's eat!" she said, giving Adam a spat on the butt as she walked to the table.

* * * * *

Libraries have a smell that is all their own. As Adam walked into the Municipal Library building, the soft, musty odor caused him to flash back to his high school days, the last

21

time that he had set foot in such a place. Perhaps the odor was from the countless sheets of paper, some decades old, that sat in majestic rows on the shelves. Maybe it was the smell of knowledge, Adam mused as he stopped to look around. His mother had been a teacher for decades before finally retiring, and she often said that every library in every town across America was a repository of the collected knowledge of man. Today Adam was banking on that. As he walked up to the massive front desk, he waited only a moment before a woman approached. Her nametag announced her as 'Marsha, Desk Librarian'.

"May I help you?" the woman named Marsha said pleasantly.

"Well, this may sound crazy, but I'm looking for some information on somebody named Saint Lucia." He shrugged. "I don't even know if she's real, but–"

Without changing her expression, the woman sighed and said, "You're probably referring to the Catholic saint whose festival day brings in the Christmas season in several countries around the world. In fact, Saint Lucia's day was yesterday."

"Okay," he said slowly, more than a little surprised. "How'd you know all that?"

"We always have a service at the church on December thirteenth. One young girl is chosen as Saint Lucia. She dresses in a white robe with a ring of candles on her head, and leads the children from the church into the sanctuary. They sing Christmas songs, tell stories, and start the season off right."

"Hmm. Okay, since I don't know anything about Saint Lucia's Day and I'd like to find out more, do you have any suggestions?"

Marsha pointed to a row of archaic computer terminals on a table across the lobby. "Go to any one of those terminals and type in 'Lucia' and 'Christmas' and you'll get a list of references."

"Great. Thanks," he said, and walked over to the first terminal. Five minutes later, Adam was wandering the corridors of the non-fiction room with a list of reference books in his hand. He wanted to find whatever he could, and then get back to the grocery store to see Emily so that she wouldn't become even more suspicious. He let out a sigh. He had also volunteered to pick up Amy after school, and then to prepare dinner. It was going to be a busy day, but Adam could think of no better way to spend it. If Lucia was right, then every hour with his family – no, every minute – was now critically important. He didn't know how many he had left. He felt a lump in his throat, but took a deep breath and moved on.

* * * * *

It was dark and cold. Adam had been standing on the porch for half an hour. Sleep had been sparse, filled with thoughts and dreams that would not let him rest. After several hours of trying, Adam finally slipped out of bed and walked into the den, where he had left his clothes so that he could dress without waking Emily. On the way out he stepped into his daughter's room, pulled the covers up around her, and kissed her forehead. He then went out to meet Lucia, with his question for the evening prepared. Elvis was sprawled on the ground at his feet. Now, however, he was starting to feel a bit silly.

He sighed. "I could have sworn it wasn't a dream," Adam said to himself. He shook his head at his own foolishness, and then started back into the house.

"It was not a dream, Adam," said a soft voice behind him. He quickly turned to see Lucia standing on the edge of the porch, looking pristine and radiant, exactly as she had appeared the night before. The evening had exploded with light. Elvis jumped up, putting his front paws on her waist and giving a

23

low groan as he stretched against her. She rubbed the top of his head and tussled his floppy ears.

"I didn't think you were coming. I guess I was starting to think that you weren't real," Adam said.

"Of course I am real. You waited so long to call me that I thought you might be collecting your thoughts before we spoke."

"Sorry. I've been wondering all day if last night was all a dream, and I guess I was becoming convinced that it was."

Lucia stopped rubbing the basset, and he plopped his front feet to the ground. She walked over to the edge of the patio, sat on a wooden bench, and folded her hands on her lap. "Are you ready to ask this evening's question?" she asked.

Adam looked into her eyes, and marveled at how deep they were. They seemed to contain a mix of ultimate knowledge and absolute peace. "Before you answer my question, are we allowed to just talk for a bit?"

"Of course."

"So I hear that you're a Catholic saint. I even checked out a few books about you, although I haven't had a chance to read them all yet. From what I skimmed, though, you must be Saint Lucia, patron saint of the blind. Oddly enough, it said that you were Italian. It surprised me because you seem to keep popping up in other books I found about Christmas in the Scandinavian countries."

Lucia nodded her head. "All that is true," she said, a smile crossing her lips. "It is a story in itself."

"Ah. Anyway, I ended up with several books to read."

"Why are you so interested in me?"

"Let's see. A saint or spirit or ghost or whatever you are shows up in my backyard to tell me that I'm about to die, offers to help me work through this fear of death that I've always had, acts like that will somehow make everything okay, and you wonder why I'm curious?"

24

"It was never my intent to unsettle you so. I hope that–"

"Oh wait, no, I'm glad that you're here" Adam interrupted. "If I have to die now, which I'm still not sure of, I guess I'm supposed to get a preview of what I have to face." He stopped, and walked over to the edge of the patio, looking out at the stars. "I started to tell Emily. I – I didn't know how well she could handle it. Throughout the day, I've wondered how well I'm handling it." Tears welled up in his eyes, and a solitary drop rolled down his cheek. He was silent for a long time, before finally turning around to face the girl. "One minute it feels like I've been hit in the stomach with a baseball bat, and the next it's so surreal that I can't even imagine that it's true. I spent half the day thinking that this was all a dream – or a nightmare – and the other half trying not to let Emily see me cry. At other times, I'm almost giddy because I'm getting to spend some extra time with my family. I feel like I'm a yo-yo, going up and down, and up and down."

"Do not be afraid, Adam. I am here to help you understand. Also, it is not my wish that you are to die; it is simply the way of things. Most people never have a chance to prepare, or at least do not take it when it appears. My task is to help you do just that. Tonight you will be given your first explanation of death," Lucia said softly. "And with that, what is the question that I may answer?" She sat there serenely, the halo of light a severe contrast to the darkness of night.

"I've spent some time thinking about this. Trying to decide what the strongest fear that I have about dying really is. I think that the first question is this: How does it feel to die?"

"Ah, a question of the physical body." Lucia looked momentarily up, and then smiled back at Adam. "Your faith is stronger than you know. Multitudes wrestle daily with questions of their destination. You instead are worried about the physical sensation. Good. I'll simply answer this: it is beautiful."

25

Adam wrinkled his brow. "Beautiful? I'm asking about a feeling, Lucia. I don't understand what you're saying."

The girl reached up and pushed her hair back from her face, pausing in thought. Finally, she looked up at Adam. "Over the days that we have together, I will have to take answers that are far beyond your ability to understand and put them in much simpler terms. For instance, consider the vehicle that you were traveling in when I first saw you on the road. It is a complex piece of machinery that even you don't completely understand. Now suppose that your daughter asked how it worked. You would not refer her to huge manuscripts with detailed information. Instead, you would seek to give her general ideas that would satisfy her now, but that she could also use as a foundation for a more thorough understanding later when she is able. That is exactly what I must do with you, Adam. It is literally beyond the ability of the human mind to understand the ways of the universe - God's ways." She paused again, and then continued. "I sense wonderful memories from your childhood. Think back to that first day of summer, when your school was finally dismissed. Do you remember swimming?"

Adam flashed back to those wonderful days, a feeling of warmth and security from his youth. "Oh yes. Dave and Jason, Roy and I - we'd head for old man Darden's pasture and the huge pond there." He stopped speaking, as his mind took him back to that time.

"There was something liberating about that first time you jumped into the water, no?"

"Oh, Lucia, we'd go so far as to make ourselves wait for it. Even though we could have been swimming for weeks, we'd stay away from the pond so that the first time we jumped in, we'd be free from school." A laugh escaped his lips, as he shook his head from side to side, reveling in the memory.

"Please describe it to me," she said.

"Well, I'd crawl through the barb-wire fence, and when I was clear I'd start running across the field. As I ran, I'd pull off my shirt, then socks and shoes as I hopped along, and finally my pants just as I hit the pond. With a lunge from the very edge, I'd jump to the middle where I knew it was deep enough to land. Wow. I can feel it right now, Lucia. The air was warm, and I'd feel it rushing around me as I jumped, then I'd hit the water that I now know is fed from an underground spring. For only the smallest instant, I'd be freezing. But then my body would sync with the water and it was the most perfect sensation of the entire summer. Oh my, Lucia, it was…"

"Beautiful?" she finished for him.

Adam smiled, nodded his head, and said "Yes, beautiful. Okay, I see what you mean."

"It is more than just understanding my description, Adam. It is understanding yours. Death is exactly like that. You are out of the water and warm, then you are engulfed in its coolness and feel a comfort beyond description. That is how it feels to die. When the time comes, you will feel exactly what you described, and although you will be flooded with a thousand sensations and feelings, for a brief instant you will take the time to think 'It was exactly how Lucia and I discussed'."

Adam was silent for some time. Finally, he said, "I'll have to think about this, Lucia. I'll need time to digest it."

"I know. It is a difficult concept. One second you are alive, and in the next moment your heart stops and you are slipping away. But it is exactly like jumping into the water. Never forget that." After a moment she said, "Your first question was easy. I trust that they will become more difficult as we go. I will see you tomorrow evening." She smiled, and turned to walk away. After only a few yards, she turned back to face him. "My death was horrible by human terms, Adam. It was tortuous and violent. Yet for me, the sensation was the same.

27

After a moment of the pain of this world, I was embraced in the next."

"Right, and you haven't told me how I'm going to die; what if it is in a twisted, burning car accident, or stabbed by a burglar here at the house. I read a little about your death in one of those books – it was terrible. You were burned, blinded, and run though with a sword!"

She stopped for a moment, looking out into the darkness of the night. Turning back to him, she said, "All that is true, but it wasn't that different from human birth. When you were in your mother's womb everything was warm and secure. Your mother's heartbeat played like a lullaby for you, and you thought that it was the most perfect of all places. Remember that, Adam?"

"Being in my mother's womb? Of course not."

Lucia smiled. "Still, you were there. Trust me. But when the time came for your birth, it was a shocking experience – the fluids that you so serenely floated in drained away, and you were forced through the birth canal by pressure that you'd never felt before. In this new world for you the light was almost blinding, a doctor held you upside down and smacked your bottom to make you cry to clear your windpipe, and from that point on your life began to unfold before you."

Adam shrugged. "Okay – and your point is?"

"I went through pain, but then found myself in a wonderful new world. You would never give up this world to go back to the womb, no matter how wonderful you found it to be there. In spite of my terrible end, I had so many joyous times in my life. But I would never give up the world that I live in now, not for any reason or temptation. Don't fear it, Adam," she concluded. Lucia turned, and walked away into the distance.

Adam stood there for quite some time without moving. He thought again and again about her words. Finally, Elvis stood up, stretched, and walked over to poke at Adam's feet with his nose.

"Ready to go in, boy? I think I am, too," he said, and followed the basset into the house. Adam took a quick glance to make sure that Elvis' bowl was full of water. He walked by his daughter's room and tucked the covers around her, then took off his sweatshirt and jeans and crawled into bed beside Emily. Before falling asleep, he leaned over and kissed her. "I love you, babe," he whispered. Even in her sleep, she smiled.

The Third Day

Friday, December 15th

Adam was in that groggy stage of half-sleep, where consciousness had only taken a partial grasp. He could feel the daylight streaming in from behind the curtains of the bedroom. Sounds from their dressing room told him that Emily was already up, and with a great deal of effort Adam flopped his right hand over to her side of the bed to find it empty.

"So I see you're finally up," she said, standing in the large doorway between their bedroom and dressing area. "'Bout time. I had already decided that we weren't going to get treated to another wonderful breakfast this morning."

"Morning" he said rubbing his eyes. "What time is it?"

"It's seven. I was going to let you sleep in."

"No way!" he said, swinging his feet from under the covers to the side of the bed. "I still have time to make a quick breakfast. Like I said yesterday, I want to spend every possible minute with the two of you."

"Well get to it, mister. I've got to get out of here soon, and your daughter's got a bus to catch."

31

"I'll take her to school. Then I'll come by the store and see you. After that I'm going to get the oil changed in the truck, get a physical, and then I'll meet you back here."

Emily stopped in her tracks. "You're going to what?" she said, almost accusingly.

"Get the oil changed in–"

"No, the physical. I've been after you for ten years to go get one. Now you take two weeks off from work, and for some reason decide that it's a good idea to go to the doctor. What's wrong, Adam?" she asked sternly.

"Nothing. Trust me. I'm just trying to tie up all the loose ends for the year." He walked into the dressing area of their bedroom, swatting her on her bottom as he walked by. "For once I do something that you ask me to, and you give me all this grief," he said, trying to sound like he was teasing.

"Well, okay," she said suspiciously. "Let's go get that breakfast going. But I'm still not convinced. You'd better come straight to the store after you get through with the doctor and tell me what he says."

"Done. C'mon!" he replied, racing her into the hallway and through to the kitchen.

* * * * *

Adam felt uncomfortable. "Doc," he said, "are we almost through? The thin paper on this leather table's making my butt itch." He sat with his feet dangling over the edge of the examination table of the town's only doctor.

"The paper's there for your protection, son, so either stand up and walk around or reach back and scratch that butt," the old doctor said in a monotone as he continued to write in Adam's folder.

Adam took his advice and hopped off the table, holding his arms behind him to close the gap in the gown. He paced in front of the table, waiting impatiently for a word from the doctor. Finally, the old man clicked the end of his pen, returned it to his pocket and shut the manila folder.

"Well?" Adam asked.

"Adam." the doctor said, trailing off with a sigh. "I can't believe that it was over three decades ago that your dad called me in the middle of the night, and I hopped into my car and followed behind him and your mother all the way to the hospital for you to be born. I smacked that bottom of yours good when you came out, and over the years I wonder if I shouldn't have given you a better whack to get you started. But I got you through acne, got Emily through her first period, got you through your prostate infection, got Emily over that scare over the lump in her breast, delivered Amy, saw all of you through a hundred bouts of colds, the flu and a virus here and there."

"Doc, I know–" Adam tried to interrupt.

"Not to mention everything else," the doctor continued, overriding Adam, "and just when I thought that I was going to retire and watch you and yours grow old, you march in here and tell me that you're dying." He eyed Adam from forehead to toe, then shook his head. "Hell, boy, I'm seventy years old next year, and I'd give anything to be in the shape you're in. You could lose a pound or two, maybe tell Emily to quit baking those incredible apple pies that she does, but other than that, you're the picture of health."

It was Adam's turn to shake his head. He said, "Look doc, I'm telling you that something is wrong. I'm about to check out, but I want to know why. And how."

"So, Doctor Adam," he replied with a voice thick with sarcasm, "how did you arrive at this prognosis, when it escapes a simple country doctor such as myself?"

Adam stopped for a moment, sure that if he told the truth about Lucia that the doctor would put him in the hospital all right – a mental hospital. "I – I had a dream," he lied. "But it was the kind of dream that you know is going to come true. Something is wrong with me, doc, and in the next two weeks I'm going to die. You have to help me discover what it is so that I can be prepared."

"Adam, you're not going to die. Trust me. You're most likely going to be attending my funeral, in fact... although I hope that it's a few decades away."

"Doc, you have to look closer. You have to do something. I'm positive about this. I really am." He almost sounded desperate.

The doctor studied him. After a long silence, the doctor nodded his head. "Okay, Adam, I think I have something that will help you out." He pulled a prescription pad from his white jacket, and began scratching on it. He finally tore off the top sheet and handed it to Adam. "Fill this, follow the directions, and if you are still certain that you're dying we'll go from there."

He took the prescription, folded it and inserted it into his pocket of his shirt draped over a chair. "Thanks doc. I'll let you know how it works." Adam reached out to shake his hand, which the doctor did solemnly. As the old man left the room, Adam shed the gown and began to get dressed.

When he stopped at the receptionist's desk, Carla waved him on. "He says not to charge you for this one, Adam. Looks like you're getting off cheap."

He smiled at the girl and said, "Tell the doc that I said 'thanks' and that I owe him one," as he pushed open the door. The brisk December air immediately chilled him as he dashed across the parking lot and stepped across Main Street. There was no traffic, and the downtown block was almost deserted. After a few steps he reached the door of the town pharmacy and stepped inside to the warmth.

"'Morning, Adam," Mrs. Kelsey called from behind the counter.

Adam waved. She had worked at the pharmacy for as long as he could remember, and had rung up every prescription that he'd ever had filled on the antiquated register on the counter. "Is Mr. Parks in?" he asked.

"Oh, right here, Adam," Leonard Parks said as he walked from behind one of the pharmacy shelves. The medicines were kept on an array of shelves behind a tall counter, all elevated half a foot on a raised floor. This allowed Mr. Parks, the pharmacist, to peer down at his customers while dispensing their medicines. "What can we do for you this fine holiday afternoon?"

"Got a 'script from the doc, Mr. Parks. I'd appreciate it if you could get it filled today for me," he said, walking down one of the short aisles of the store.

"Oh, shouldn't be a problem. I've already filled a dozen bottles of cough syrup today, and prescribed at least that many over-the-counter cold tablets in spite of that old coot across the street. It's a typical cold and flu season here in town."

Adam handed him the folded piece of paper from his pocket. "Proud to hear it. My only question is how you get off calling the doc an 'old coot'," he said, joking with the pharmacist.

"Hell Adam, he's seventy. I'm only sixty-five. Compared to him, I'm a spring chicken. I'm a hundred times more qualified to dispense medicine."

"You know, the doc might argue that fact," Adam said, sensing Parks' tongue-in-cheek attitude.

The pharmacist laughed out loud. "That's one of the arguments I live for," he said, smiling. "Now let's see what I can do for you." He opened the folded paper and peered at it over his glasses. After a moment of studying it, he looked at Adam. "I can't fill this prescription."

"Huh?" Adam asked, confused.

"Just what I said. I can't fill this for you."

"Mr. Parks, what did he prescribe? Is it some over-the-counter medication, or something so rare that you have to order it?" He was now genuinely concerned. Never before had the pharmacy been unable to fill a prescription. Adam feared that it was something serious indeed.

"I take it you didn't read this," Parks said, handing the paper back to Adam. "It seems that he's prescribing you a six-pack of beer. The directions are that you find a good football game on TV, sit back in your recliner and proceed to take your medication," he continued with a smirk.

"You're kidding."

"Read it for yourself."

Adam studied the prescription pad, and laughed as he nodded his head in amusement. "Well, I guess I actually can fill this one myself."

"Tell you what," Parks said. "Let me buy you a cup of coffee and you tell me all about this." He stepped down from the pharmacist's counter and walked over to the soda fountain that lined the side of the store. He pulled two cups down from a shelf stacked with the glasses, cups and bowls that were necessary to the dispensing of soft drinks and ice cream. Turning both cups mouth up on the counter, he filled each with a steaming cup of coffee from a pot that was prepared as the morning light shown into the front window and was kept going until the front door was locked. "Have a seat there, Adam," he nodded toward the white Formica table at the front window. Several chairs surrounded it, and it was a favorite gathering place for the old men in town, especially in the early morning.

Adam walked over pulled out a chair and accepted a cup from Mr. Parks. Taking a sip, he smiled and said "Good stuff. There's nothing like your fresh coffee."

Mr. Parks took a sip and nodded in agreement. He set the cup down. "Anything bothering you, young man?"

"Nothing in particular. Why?" he said, taking another sip.

"Emily comes in here to get medicine any time that one of the three of you is sick. I've heard her say more than once that she wished you go in for a physical, but you're just plain hardheaded about it. I just figured that you were scared."

He laughed at the allegation. "You know, Mr. Parks, I wish that there was some way that I could deny that. I guess that I always have been. Afraid, I mean. Afraid that the doc might tell me that I had some horrible disease or something."

"So why the sudden change of heart?" Parks asked, sipping his coffee, being careful to walk the line between prying and trying to help.

"Aw, I guess that it's because I'm looking ahead of me and I see that halfway mark right out there. I just wanted to make sure that everything was working okay right now."

Parks just stared at him, looking into his eyes questioningly.

"Okay, okay." He took a drink of coffee, feeling it warm his mouth. Struggling with how to say what he was feeling without seeming crazy, Adam finally said, "You know, Mr. Parks, I've got a computer at home on my desk. There's a program on that computer that lets us put things on a calendar that it keeps. You know, reminding us of birthdays and what-not. It will even print off a year's calendar on a page, as far in the future as you tell it to. I guess that recently I realized that I could print off about a hundred pages, each with a year's calendar on it, and I could take those pages and flip through them. And even though I couldn't see it with my eyes, there would be an invisible mark on one of those pages on a particular month and day. And that is the day that I will die. I would like to hope that the day would be fifty or sixty years

37

away. I realized, though, that it could also be tomorrow... or a couple of weeks from now."

Parks nodded, understanding. "You're right. That day is out there for all of us." He took another sip of coffee. "Death's a funny thing, you know. You're in your late thirties. I'm sixty-five, and the doc's got five more years on me. But you could leave this store, step onto the sidewalk and have a stroke hit you that had been laying in wait for years without you ever knowing about it. I could just as easily get broadsided by a truck on the highway on my next trip to the city. The driver could have fallen asleep and just take me out without any word or warning. And the doc, well, the doc could go another twenty years, or just as easily fall over tomorrow from some illness he picked up from a patient. No one has any guarantees, Adam. A lot of good people die before they're twenty-five, some even when they're born, and some of the most evil sons-of-bitches in the world grow old and gray and prosper like no one could possibly imagine. There's no rhyme or reason, no formula to it. Only God knows. I guess that if we have questions about it all, we just have to wait until we can ask him in person."

Parks started to speak again, but choked on the words and instead raised his coffee cup to his lips. They were both silent, looking out the window onto Main street, until Parks was able to continue. "You know that I lost Mary five years ago this coming February. We knew each other our entire lives. Grew up together, started growing old together, and she went and got the pneumonia. It was tough on her, but she beat it. When it relapsed, though, it sucked the very life from her. The girl I knew in pigtails, the young woman that I married and took to bed on our wedding night, the woman who helped me fret over money and mortgage and whatever else, was reduced to a weak, pale child in a hospital bed." As he spoke, a tear ran slowly down his cheek. "She could barely speak to me on the last day. We both knew that she was going to die, but it was a conversation that we'd never had before. We didn't know what to say, and certainly didn't want to waste the few moments and words that she had left. I took her hand, Adam, and I started crying. Hell, I was sobbing. All I could say to her was 'I'm sorry, Mary'. She just lightly stroked my hair, as best as she could, and told me that she loved me. She said that she knew she was about to go, but that she wasn't scared of it. 'Not scared?' I asked her. 'Well, maybe scared like Disneyland', she said. She told me that she loved me two more times, and then it sounded like she gave a long sigh. I was confused, but then I realized that it was the last air escaping from her lungs. She was gone."

"Oh, man." Adam said, shaking his head. "I – I don't know what to say. I'm sorry to bring all this back up–"

Parks raised his hand to stop him. "Hold on there, Adam. I'm not through. That's the hard part to tell. Now let me finish." He looked back over his shoulder to see that Mrs. Kelsey was out of hearing distance. "Look here, Adam," he said in a more hushed voice. "What I'm about to tell you I've never told anyone else, not even the preacher. A lot of people would think that I'm crazy, and a crazy man filling prescriptions in a little town doesn't make much money." He looked into Adam's eyes. "I'm going to need your word on this."

"You have it," Adam replied somberly. "I won't tell a soul."

He looked around again, and then continued. "I fell apart at her bedside. They came and put her body on a gurney, covered it with a sheet, and unceremoniously rolled her out. I just sat there crying. The doctor offered to give me something to knock me out, but I refused. I felt alone. I was mad at Mary for leaving and mad at God for taking her. I'm not sure that I had ever felt as desolate in my life. I'm not sure that anyone ever has. I got up and walked out of the hospital by myself. I must have looked the devil, because everyone was staring at me, but I didn't care. I drove myself home and just sat in the dark. The funeral home called. See, Mary's biggest fear about death was getting put in a box in the ground. We had already made arrangements to be cremated, and the funeral home had her body ready to be viewed before they did it. I drove down there, and looked at her body, and told them not to do it." He paused momentarily, and then shook his head as if to come back to the present. "I was sure that if I gave up her body she'd be gone forever. I guess they'd seen all that before, because they told me to go home and sleep and we'd talk again in the morning. Well, I went home, and I tried to do just that. I tried to sleep, and just drifted in and out for hours. I couldn't sleep for my mind racing, though, and I've got to be honest with you. I had almost convinced myself that Mary was just gone. That there wasn't a God, there wasn't a heaven, that Mary had just slipped away into nothing. I guess I kept hearing the air escaping her body. I realized how fragile humans really are. Nothing but flesh and bones." His gaze had drifted away from Adam as he spoke, but he turned to look squarely at him again. "See, Adam, I'm in the business of science. My degree is in pharmacy, and I can directly see the effect that different chemical compounds have on the human body. It's not hard to let your logical mind take charge and imagine that we're nothing but animals that have evolved into some kind of senescent beings. That we've come to the point that we're the only animal who can stop and think about dying, and that we've had to invent a God and an afterlife to keep us from going insane from the aspect of our world just stopping and going into nothing. Well that's where I was. In the middle of the night, though, I heard a voice – Mary's voice – calling out to me. I stood up and followed it outside, and standing there in our back yard was Mary. Not sickly and thin like I'd left her earlier, but as healthy and beautiful as I'd ever remembered her. She was that young lady that I'd first fallen in love with."

Adam swallowed hard and fought back the urge to speak.

"I said 'Mary, is that you?' and she just smiled and told me that it was. She said that she was safe and warm and happy, and that everything was perfect. I asked her why she had come back, then, and she said that God had only allowed it to help me understand. She said that it was an ultimate gift, one that God was giving me. When I asked her where she was and what it was like, she only said 'just like I said it was'. I remembered, and asked her what she meant by Disneyland there on her deathbed. She smiled and said, 'Do you remember when you took me to Disneyland after it opened? I was excited, but I was scared because I didn't know what to expect. I was afraid that the rides would be too big or whatever, but when we got there, I just loved it. It was one of my favorite vacations that we ever took. Death was the same. I was afraid, but I knew that it was going to be a powerful experience'. She smiled and I knew that she was happy. 'You're not going to believe it, dear. When you breathe your last breath, I'll be waiting. I'll personally escort you into the presence of God. He loves you so much. Don't be afraid'. She blew me a kiss, then turned and walked away." Parks pulled out a handkerchief and blew his nose.

"You know, Mr. Parks, I believe that what you saw was real," Adam said to comfort him.

"Oh hell, of course it was!" he exclaimed, a smile breaking through the tears. "When I was standing there, I noticed how cold it was, and me out there in my underwear. I thought, 'I can't be dreaming – it's cold!' but I walked around out there long enough to convince myself. I finally went back in and built a fire, then stayed awake the rest of the night just so I'd be sure that it was really Mary. When the sun came up and I was still in the same state of mind, I knew what was what. I called the funeral home and told them to go ahead with the body, that

Mary was through with it. Since that night, I haven't questioned a thing." He laughed out loud. "I can't say that I haven't gone out into the back yard in the dead of night occasionally, calling her name and hoping that she would come back again, but I know that she's somewhere doing something else, and she's very, very happy. I don't know what heaven is like, Adam, but I looked straight into those glowing eyes of hers. I saw complete and total bliss. One of these days, and that day's on your calendar you were talking about, I'm going to join her."

Adam nodded, agreeing with his statement. "I know you are." He lifted his coffee cup in a toast to the pharmacist. "Thanks, Mr. Parks. I needed to hear your story. I know that Mary came back for you, but maybe she also came back so that you could tell the story to me."

"Maybe so, Adam. I guess that I got off from our discussion a bit. I'm sorry. Every time I think of her, though, it brightens my day." He smiled and downed the last of his cup.

"I'm glad. Thanks again." Adam drained his cup as well. "I guess that I'd better be going. I promised Emily that I'd come by after the exam with a report. Besides, I have an appointment tonight, and I want to do some reading first. I guess that I've always wondered what heaven is like. Maybe I'll ask around."

"Won't help. I think that it's one of those things that you can only describe it if you've been there," Mr. Parks said, and extended his hand.

Adam shook it firmly, smiling at his own private joke. He did, in fact, know someone who had been there. "Thanks, old man. Be careful out on the highway," he said.

"Old man, my ass. Save that for someone who needs it." He laughed and stood. As he walked back behind the pharmacy counter, he was whistling.

Adam pushed the pharmacy door open and stepped into the street. He rolled his eyes skyward, and said "So, Lucia, you're not the only one that God sends on missions of rescue to troubled humans." He laughed aloud. "I'm going to find out who you were, young lady."

* * * * *

"Lucia? Are you here?" Adam called. It was once again midnight, and he was shivering in the back yard. After dinner, he and Emily had washed the dishes while their daughter watched a cartoon movie on the television. They put her to bed, watched the news, and then went to bed themselves. Emily had fallen asleep while Adam lay in bed reading a book on Catholic saints, with a section on a particular Italian saint named Lucia. He woke with the light still on and the book on his chest, and got up, realizing that it was time for their meeting.

"Lucia? Are you here?" he called again.

"Of course I am here," her voice said. It came from beside him, although there was no one there only moments before.

He turned to face her, having to momentarily shield his eyes from the bright light emanating from her. "Wow. Why are you always so bright?"

Lucia only laughed. "What may I answer you tonight, Adam?"

"I read more about you today; I had a long wait at the doctor's office, so I took one of the library books along. Good Lord, Lucia. Was the story of your death true?" he asked with amazement in his voice. "I mean, it was horrible. I can't believe a young woman – or anyone for that matter – would have to go through such an ordeal that the book described."

Her face grew solemn. "My death must seem very unpleasant. But it is not my death that is important. It is the manner in which God took it and used it. He worked a miracle.

43

It frightened the pagan Roman government, and it inspired people through the ages since. People since have held celebrations on the festival that they call Saint Lucia's Day. But it is not to honor me. It is instead to honor God and the way that he used me in my death. Don't let your books confuse you about me or who I am."

"I don't mean for them to, Lucia, and forgive me for asking, but could you tell me about your life? I knew nothing about you before you showed up here in my backyard. Since then, I've found out that you're a big part of the Christmas season, not only overseas but in various parts of America as well. God chose to send you to give me a message. I don't mean to be nosy, Lucia, but I'm understandably curious. You can even make that my question for tonight."

"With all the things you have had on your mind about death, you must sincerely want to know to waste a question on something as trivial as me." She walked over to the back porch swing and sat down. As if on cue, Elvis stuck his nose through the doggie door, looked around, then plodded over to jump into the swing beside her. She smiled as the dog reached up to nuzzle against her face. "But your gift was to be able to find the answers you seek about death. As far as I don't interfere with that, I will be happy to tell you of my life. And you may still ask the question that you have prepared for this evening."

Adam nodded his head. "Thanks," he said, and sat down into one of the wooden patio chairs across from the swing. He sat rapt in attention.

"I was born in Syracuse, Sicily in the year that you would call 283. I was an only child, and my family was rich. In those days, that translated to a very healthy dowry. Because of that, I had many suitors."

"I doubt that's the only reason," Adam interjected. "You're a very pretty girl, Lucia."

She smiled. "Thank you. But to continue… in my teenage years, my parents finally selected a husband for me. It was the son of a nobleman in the city. The marriage would be profitable for both families, it seemed. He was a nice enough boy, but I didn't really like him. I certainly didn't love him. It was also around that time that I was out at the market one day, and heard two people talking about a religion that was strange to me. It was the worship of a loving God, not like the violent gods of Rome that demanded sacrifice and offerings. I was intrigued, and followed the men at a distance, listening to them. They finally saw me, and started to flee. I caught up to them, and finally convinced them that I was not an agent of the government. They agreed to tell me more, and I met with them and some of their friends several more times. I embraced the Christian faith, and began sneaking out of my home to attend regular meetings."

"Hold on. Why would they think that you were a government spy?" Adam asked, confused by the turn of events in her story.

"The times were very different than in your country today, Adam. All other religions were illegal. Only the gods of Rome could be worshipped. And you had to worship those gods under penalty of death. You see, I had heard of the Christian faith but I did not know anything about it. My family and I blindly made sacrifices and offerings to the Roman gods."

"Wow. I can't even imagine a society like that. I think that in today's world people would rebel," he said thoughtfully.

"Do not be too quick to your conclusion, Adam. It is true that you have far more freedom of religion than any other place or time. But people are imperfect. They unknowingly corrupt even the most precious things. There are parts of the world where wars are started over the sole point of religion. In another part of the world, Christians fight among themselves, with Catholics and Protestants taking up arms against one another. In your own country people have become so convinced that they have the one and only faith that they insist on forcing their morals and beliefs on everyone else." She stopped talking and petted the basset hound beside her in the swing. After he groaned his approval, she continued. "As time passed, I found myself more and more in the service of God. When I was to meet with my betrothed, I would instead be with my group serving food that we had gathered to the poor. One day, I came home to find my betrothed waiting at my home with my parents. The all pressed for an explanation, so I told them of my Christian faith."

"Oops."

"Indeed. My father was outraged, and forbade me to meet with the Christian group again. He promised my betrothed that he would put an end to 'this madness' as he called it. Unfortunately, I let my anger rise, and renounced my parents. I told them that I would no longer live in their home, and told my betrothed that I would die before marrying him. He left in a rage, and went straight to the city's governing house and asked for an audience with Paschasius, our local governor. He reported my Christian faith to him, and even as I was still arguing with my parents, the soldiers came for me."

"Wow," Adam said. "It must have felt like the entire world was against you. I can only imagine how scared you must have been."

"Terrified. My mother wept uncontrollably, and my father pleaded with the soldiers to let him handle the situation. They wouldn't listen, of course, and led me through the streets, with my betrothed following behind calling me unspeakable names. When I was finally presented to the governor, he told me that I had to offer a public sacrifice to the Roman gods or I would be sentenced. I denounced the gods as false, and claimed only the salvation of the Christian God. My father tried to bargain with Paschasius for my freedom, but the best that he could do was to buy my life. Instead of a death sentence, I was ordered to be given over to a brothel, where I would have to live a life of prostitution. My mother was crying so hard that she started gasping for air, and finally fainted." Lucia softly trailed off her story.

"Hey, if this is bringing back some bad memories, then by all means–"

"There are no bad memories," Lucia said softly. She had stopped stroking Elvis' neck, and he let out a low groan to show his disapproval. With his nose, he gently nudged her hand. "I am sorry, Adam. I just got caught up in my own thoughts. And I am sorry to you, too" she said, looking down at the dog and scratching his head. "I did not realize you were so insistent!"

"He's probably the most spoiled dog on the planet. If he gets to be a bother, just push him down."

"No bother at all. It is a pleasure, in fact. So back to my story," she continued. "I told the governor that he did not have the right to punish me for my Christian beliefs. This only angered him, and he ordered the soldiers to take me away. I stood there and closed my eyes, praying harder and with more conviction than I had ever prayed before. I felt the solders grab my arms, but that was it. After a few moments, I opened my eyes, and there were two grown men – two strong soldiers – trying with all their might to move me. Yet I stood there immovable before Paschasius."

"How is that possible?" he asked. "Were you straining against them, or what?"

She shook her head. "No, I was doing nothing but standing there. Somehow God was not allowing me to be moved. I did not feel the slightest pressure of their attempts. This went on for quite some time. Various men tried, but none were able. I stood there, praying. The terror that I had felt up to that point had passed, though. It was replaced by a calm, a peace that I had never felt before. I was no long afraid, even when I heard the governor order that I be burned where I stood. They piled wood around me as if I were fixed to a stake, and then lit the fire. I did not understand how, but I was still had no fear. As the minutes passed, I opened my eyes again, and saw that I was not being consumed by the flame. The people in the hall were silent, all staring in disbelief."

Adam wrinkled his brow. "Didn't it hurt?"

"No. It was like passing your hand quickly though a flame. You can feel the flame licking your skin, feel its tingle and its heat, but you are unharmed. That is exactly how it was with me. The wood around me burned, but not me. Not even my hair or clothes. Finally, one of the soldiers walked over to face me, kicked away the burning wood around me, drew his sword, and ran me through. It was then that I died."

Adam sat in silence for a moment, and finally asked, "How did it feel to die like that?"

"The blade jerked my body when it entered. After that, there was a pain that shot all the way through me. Things around the room begin to fade, and then if felt exactly as we talked about last night." Lucia paused for a moment. "As if I had taken an early summer plunge into Darden's pond," she then said, smiling at Adam.

He found a world of comfort in that smile. "Thank you, Lucia. I didn't mean to get you off on such a long story, but it was fascinating. One question, though. Why did the sword kill you after everything else that had happened?"

"I was to die that day, but God was able to use my death as a message to Paschasius and the others who were there. The stories of it also rippled though the country, igniting the fire of the Christian faith more. The reason that I died by the sword is simply that God had finished his message. Prolonging it would not have made any more of an impression. And only moments after the sword pierced me, I was embraced by God himself in a feeling of warmth and love like I never knew was possible."

Adam took a deep breath. "I – I don't know what to say. Wow."

Lucia laughed. "Well said, Adam. God's power is awesome. Now turning to you, and the reason that I am here, what can I tell you about death tonight?"

He paused, staring off into the night as he contemplated Lucia's story. Finally, he turned to face her. "I've been trying to think of what I'm afraid of when it comes to dying. You helped a lot last night."

Lucia nodded her head once, and smiled warmly.

"But after talking to a friend of mine today, I've got a question that's more about what happens after I die. Lucia, tell me what heaven is like."

Lucia paused briefly. "That's one that I wouldn't have anticipated. Most people have their own vision of what heaven is. They are usually more preoccupied with how they are going to get there."

"Ah, maybe I can explain. See, I have a couple of images of heaven that I've been carrying around all these years, and I've never been too comfortable with them."

"And these images are?" Lucia asked softly.

"Both of them are from sitting in the church listening to the preacher. He was delivering a sermon on heaven, and he talked about how glorious it was: streets paved with gold, mansions of precious metals and jewels, and how everyone would have one of these mansions. At the time, I couldn't see the attraction of that. In fact, it sounded pretty dumb to me. But the more I grew, the more I remembered that image, and the more I wondered what the big deal was."

"That would be because you are not a man impressed by money or wealth. I see in your heart that you would rather live on the streets in poverty with your family than live in the finest castle without them, and that you would spend your last penny to save the life of this dog that sits beside me." As she spoke, Elvis looked up as if on cue.

"Come on," he scoffed. "My family is more important than any amount of wealth or money."

"To your credit. Still, you are a human. Mankind has always been driven by visions of wealth, and those images were used in the Bible to convey how precious heaven is. When a prophet appeared, he was often adorned with gold and wealth. The book of Revelation is full of similar images. But remember our conversation from last evening. How would you describe something to your daughter that was beyond the understanding of her young mind? You would use images that she could grasp, and use them to teach her. That is what God has done in the Bible to teach mankind, and certainly where your minister chose his illustration. But there is no material wealth in heaven, Adam. There is not even a concept of such. Drive that from your mind. So what is your other image?"

"Choir lofts."

"Choir lofts?" she asked, confused. "I do not understand."

"It was another time, and another preacher was giving a sermon on heaven. He said that heaven was filled with huge choir lofts and that we would all be sitting in them singing hymns forever. For all eternity. When I heard that, I couldn't even imagine anything more boring. It took me a long time to get over that one – there was no way that I wanted any part of heaven." Adam shrugged and raised his eyebrows. "Understand?"

Lucia nodded, and said "Perfectly. Even then, you were looking for a concrete picture of heaven. You wanted to know exactly what you were getting into, and you were presented with symbols that held little meaning for you. It is up to me, then, to describe heaven for you." She was silent for a long time, looking him straight in the eye.

"Lucia?" he finally asked.

After a pause, she finally spoke. "Tell me the truth, Adam. Why did you ask this question?"

Adam stopped to think momentarily, and answered, "It's just something that's always bothered me. After, you know, the picture I'd been painted of heaven at church. Why?"

She continued to stare at him. "I'll ask again, Adam – tell me the truth. Why are you concerned about what heaven is like?"

"Lucia, I – I just want to know. That's no crime. Everyone wonders about it. Besides, you gave me the chance to ask whatever I–"

"I gave you nothing," she interrupted, her gaze never wavering. "God alone can give such gifts. I am but a simple messenger. But you still have not told me why it is so important to you. Tell me, Adam."

"But I have! All I asked–"

"Tell me!" Lucia said firmly.

Adam's eyes welled up with tears, and a hushed sob escaped his lips. He turned away from the girl, walking to the edge of the patio. As he composed himself, he looked up at the thousands of stars in the night sky. He knew what she was pushing for. Lucia had touched a well-hidden nerve that he did not want to expose. Finally, he turned to face Lucia again. "I'm afraid that I won't like it. I'm afraid that I'll have to spend eternity in some place that I hate, and I'll be the only one who feels like that, and–"

Lucia broke his sentence with a gentle laugh. "So there it is. Was it that hard to admit?"

He stood before her, tears still rolling down his cheeks. "I love God, Lucia. I mean, I'm not religious, and I don't pray as often as I should..."

"As I have said before, He knows your heart."

"But how do I have the right to stand here and say that heaven might not be that enjoyable for me? How can I say that to him?"

"You just did. But do not concern yourself. Let me be even clearer: God knows your heart better than you do. Perhaps he has seen your struggle with this question, and that is one of the reasons why he is allowing you this glimpse into your pending death. It is the very realization that you were worried about heaven that you needed to deal with. Now that you have taken that step, let me present you with a few questions. First of all, let me ask you about your daughter. Would you prefer to return to the time when she was an infant?"

"Would I? Well, it's been so wonderful that I wouldn't mind re-living all this time again. But I have to admit, I would rather live in the present with her. She's old enough that she's developed a wonderful personality. She's starting to experience the world and I'm getting to see it all through her eyes. Does that make sense?"

"Perfect sense. But let me ask you another question. Would you rather live in your world today or return to the time when you were not married?" Lucia asked.

"Of course not! Emily and I have been together forever. I can't even remember life without her."

"Exactly. Another question, and you may have to think back: would you rather return to the time when you were going to college, or back further to when you were in high school?"

"Hmmm." he said aloud, reaching back across the years to remember. It took only a moment before Adam spoke. "You know, I remember going to college. I had the freedom to make my own schedule, take the classes I wanted to, and determine my own destiny. No way would I have gone back to high school."

"Now. A final question" Lucia said, her voice soft and hushed. "How did you feel before each transition?"

"Apprehensive, I guess. I remember sitting in my high school graduation listening to the speaker. Some big-time lawyer. Everyone was anxious for the whole thing to be over, looking forward to the parties, and just being graduates. I couldn't wait to put my tassel on the rearview mirror of my car. But then he started talking about what each of us would be doing in the next few months, and well, it gave me the creeps. All of a sudden I realized that I wouldn't be coming back to the familiar turf or going through the motions that I was so accustomed to." Adam stopped, and then smiled at Lucia. "Okay, I see where you're going. In every case that I mentioned I felt afraid of the change, and remorse at the old life that I was giving up. You're going to tell me that the transition between this life and the next is the same."

Lucia nodded. "I only wish that I had a way to express the magnitude of the difference. At each point of transition in your life, you made it through only to look back and wonder why you would have ever been afraid. If I were able to show you a vision of heaven, it would overwhelm you with its limitless beauty. Were you to spend only a moment there before coming back, you would go mad at how bound your soul is on earth." Lucia gave Elvis a final pat on the neck, then stood and walked across the patio to Adam. As her face became solemn, she took his hands in hers. "Adam, heaven is a place so beautiful that you cannot comprehend it. There are no cities, no automobiles, no television, no internet, none of the things that comprise your life today. There are also no bills, no sickness, no crime, and no hate. It is so far beyond all that. But since your mind is limited for now, you will just have to consider it in terms that you understand." She smiled knowingly, and said, "Think of the most beautiful, most perfect feeling and place that you can imagine. Whatever that might be, it is truly an order of magnitude better than that." She let go his hands, and gently touched his forehead with her index finger. "You are going to love it, Adam."

The sensation was magnificent. A perfect peace flooded Adam's body, and he felt for a moment like he had been allowed to view heaven from a distance. His eyes had closed together, and every muscle in his body tightened. As he relaxed, and finally opened his eyes, he was alone in the darkness on his patio. A few feet away, the wooden swing rocked gently with Elvis as its only occupant. Lucia was gone, and for the first time Adam did not fear dying. He did not fear the actual event, and he trusted his destination. "Thank you, Lucia," he said out loud, and to himself thanked God, then paused to marvel at the wonders of the evening sky. A low moan came from Elvis, who was adjusting for a serious nap.

The Fourth Day

"Hello? Honey?" Emily said, confused and a little worried. When she had left to take Amy to the Bowden's, Adam had been washing the breakfast dishes and the house was alive. The house was now quiet and dark. The shades were all pulled, the curtains drawn, and every light was turned off. "Adam?" she called again.

"Did you get Amy squared away?" Adam's voice called from their bedroom down the hall.

"Yes. They're on their way to the outlet mall, which is a couple of hours away. She and Melissa were laughing and having a great time when I left. Gerry and Paula are going to take them shopping all day then drive them around and look at the Christmas lights. It'll be a full day. Paula said they'd drop her off tomorrow afternoon."

"Perfect. Can you come in here a sec?"

Emily set her purse on a chair as she passed through the den, and as she walked into the hallway she saw something unfamiliar. There was a small narrow table beside their door that was usually covered with family photographs. Its top was

55

now empty, with the exception of a white candle providing the only light in the hallway. On the table beside the candle lay a single red rose. "Adam?" she said, cautiously walking down the hallway. When she was finally able to peek around the door into their bedroom, she saw that it was bathed in candlelight. Candles of all shapes and sizes seemed to rest in every corner and on any flat surface. On her nightstand was a vase filled with beautiful crimson roses. A playfully suspicious smile crossed her lips as she took the single rose from the hall table. She smelled its sweet aroma. "What have you done?" she asked, trying to locate Adam.

"Oh, it's not often that we get the house to ourselves. I just thought that we'd take advantage of it" he said, stepping out of the dressing area of their bedroom in a white terrycloth bathrobe. In one hand he held two fluted glasses by their stems. In the other was a bottle of champagne. "Follow me," he said, using his head to gesture back into the dressing room.

Emily inhaled the aroma of the rose deeply, and then walked in after her husband. Their dressing area was combined with their bathroom, which together was easily half as large as the bedroom itself. A huge closet accounted for one wall, with mirrored doors that not only aided in the process of getting dressed in the morning but also made the room appear bigger. Another wall had a huge mirror above two sinks. One for Adam, the other for Emily. The bathroom was to one side of that, and was the one part of the house where they had splurged during construction. A large walk-in shower was in one corner, and in the other was an over-sized oval tub, equipped with Jacuzzi jets and easily large enough for two people. As in the bedroom, candles had been placed on the counters and corners, with a rose laid here and there to accent the atmosphere. The candlelight reflected in the mirrors, adding to the intimacy of the setting.

As Emily saw it, she gasped. "Oh, Adam" she said, and was unable to suppress a giggle. "This is... well, I can't describe it!"

"You're blushing," he said playfully. As she walked around the room stopping to look at a candle here or a rose there, Adam had opened the champagne and was pouring two glasses.

"I know!" she laughed. "But I can't help myself. What in the world have you done?" She had stopped in the middle of the room, stunned.

Adam handed her a glass, then leaned in to give her a soft, gentle kiss on the cheek. "To us," he said, clinking the rim of his glass with hers. He took a sip from the glass, never looking away from her eyes.

Her eyes darted around, almost embarrassed. "Adam," she said in a hushed voice, "it's barely ten in the morning!" She paused, and then took a sip from her glass, feeling delightfully sinful.

"True enough, but I've taken care of everything. I called the store while you were gone and told Alice that we would be out of pocket for the day and to handle anything that came up. She's been the assistant manager for a long time, and you know that she'll head off any problems. And Amy's safe with Gerry and Paula. You know how paranoid they are about their own kids, so they'll take great care of her." He set his glass on the vanity, and then walked around behind her. With one hand he swept her hair to one side, and softly kissed her neck. With the other, he reached around and began unbuttoning her blouse.

"So you really have taken care of everything," she said, and turned her head to kiss him. Their lips met, and then parted. "And we have the whole day to play?"

"That's right. I've even drawn a bath for us, and in the 'fridge I've got a plate of strawberries and cream. We have to keep up our strength, you know." Adam said, helping her slide out of her shirt.

"Tell you what, mister" Emily said playfully, softly kissing her husband again. "Why don't you go sample the strawberries and give a girl a moment to freshen up. I'll meet you in the tub in a second."

"Deal." Adam smiled. As he walked into the darkness of the hallway, a tear formed in the corner of one eye. He was in love and could not believe how happy they were. It was unreal to him that he was going to die and lose it all. He also felt a small pain of guilt that they had so often let the hectic day-to-day schedules crowd out the romance in their marriage. Adam opened the refrigerator door, then stopped and sighed. He had wrestled with whether or not to tell Emily about what was going to happen. He didn't know how to explain it, though, in a way that she could understand all the emotions inside him. He was still afraid, even though Lucia had alleviated some of the fear, and he couldn't bear the thought of leaving his family behind. He had decided not to tell her, at least today. Today he wanted to have a romantic day for just the two of them.

Satisfied with his decision, he lifted the plate of strawberries from the cold shelf. He had earlier spooned a small mound of cream onto the plate, so it was ready to accompany the champagne. After closing the refrigerator door, Adam brushed any trace of a tear from his eye and went to join his wife.

* * * * *

It was pitch black in the bedroom.

A strange sound woke Adam. He opened his eyes and looked at the clock on his nightstand. The digits showed two-fifteen, but he didn't know whether it was afternoon or morning. At some point, they had extinguished the candles, so the room was dark. After a moment of letting his eyes focus, he saw traces of sunlight coming in from around the window shades. "Emily?" he said softly.

Emily opened her eyes. They were snuggled together in a tangle of covers. "Ummmm, don't you dare wake me. I want to stay like this forever."

"Me too, but hang on – do you hear something?" Adam listened closely, and heard a soft, rhythmic sound somewhere between a scratching and slapping.

"Yes, I do. What the heck is it?" she wrinkled her brow, trying to determine its origin.

Suddenly a thought crossed Adam's mind. "Did we leave any of the strawberries?"

"A few, I think. They're on the plate on the side of the tub." Their heads turned toward each other in unison, and together they said "Elvis."

"He's licking up the cream, I bet." Adam turned toward the dressing room. "Elvis!" he called.

The sound stopped, and slowly the basset's head peeked from around the door. The ears drooped low, almost touching the floor. His brown and white muzzle was covered in flecks of red strawberry and smeared with cream.

"Great. I'll get him cleaned up." Before climbing out of bed, he leaned over and kissed Emily. "That was wonderful."

"You're telling me. What time is it?"

"A little after two in the afternoon. I guess we slept for a couple of hours."

"We earned it," she said, grabbing him around the waist as he was sitting up in bed. Emily pulled him back down to face her, pressing their bodies against one another under the covers. "I figure that Elvis has already gone through whatever we left on the plate."

"Well, probably," Adam reasoned.

59

"And he'll lick most of that stuff off his mouth by the time you could get a towel."

Adam nodded, putting his arms around Emily. "Oh, I'd say so."

"Then why don't we just let him continue with his party, and we'll continue with ours!" she said, pushing him onto his back and rolling over on him.

"I love the way you think, lady."

* * * * *

It was pitch black in the bedroom.

"Adam?" she said softly, opening her eyes. "Adam, wake up."

"Huh?" he replied groggily. "What time is it?"

"C'mon, Adam, wake up." Her arms were draped around him, so she put a hand on his shoulder and gently shook him.

He opened his eyes, heaved a long, relaxed breath and turned to look at her. "Hey, beautiful."

"It's too dark for you to see me, but I doubt that I'm very beautiful at the moment. We've been asleep for God knows how long. What time is it anyway?"

Adam turned his head to look at the clock. "Seven-thirty."

"Wow. How long have we been out?"

"I don't know," he said playfully. "How long were we making love?"

She shook her head. "You know, I have absolutely no idea."

"I got up about six to go to the bathroom. I made sure that all the candles were out and that Elvis was okay."

"Yeah, I was up before that. We can't lie here forever, you know. What's next?" she asked.

He pulled Emily into his arms. "Oh, I don't know. Care to..."

"No!" she said and laughed. "My goodness, Sir, how you do carry on!" she added in her best southern belle imitation.

"I've got another idea, then. Why don't you spread a blanket out on the carpet, light some of these candles, and I'll go pop a frozen pizza into the oven. We can find an old movie on the TV and have a picnic right here."

"I love it. How long will it take you to get the pizza going?"

"Meet you back here in five minutes!" Adam said, giving Emily a quick peck on the forehead then swinging his legs around onto the floor.

As he rounded the corner into the hallway, Emily called out "Bring the cable guide!"

"Got it," he replied working his way through the dark house.

* * * * *

When Adam woke again, the television was blaring with re-runs of a 1960's sit-com. He looked over at Emily, who was fast asleep. After eating most of a large pepperoni pizza, they had bundled up at the foot of the bed and apparently fallen asleep during the movie. He looked around at the clock: twelve-twenty.

"Come on, babe," he whispered, gently freeing himself from their embrace. He kneeled beside her and gently slipped his arms under her back and legs, then stood and lifted her to the bed. She stirred only a bit as he untangled the sheet and cover from their make-shift nest on the floor, then covered her with them. He kissed her on the cheek, tucking her in, and then walked into their dressing room to quietly find clothes.

As he walked by, Adam turned down the television to a whisper, afraid that a change to complete silence would be a significant enough difference to wake her. He stooped to pick up the pizza tray, and noticing that it was empty, looked around the room. Elvis was lounging in the dead center of their dressing room. "You?" he asked the dog in a hushed voice, pointing to the tray. Elvis' tail only thumped the floor in response.

He chuckled, put the tray on the vanity, and fished a pair of jeans and a sweatshirt from inside the closet. He got dressed quickly, then bent down to scratch the dog's stomach. "I don't think the vet would approve of your diet today, mutt," he said lovingly. The tail continued to rhythmically thump the floor.

Adam took a final glance to make sure that Emily was still asleep, then silently navigated through the house to the patio door. As his foot touched down on the concrete, the air in front of him instantly shone with a brilliant light.

"Hello, Adam," the beautiful voice said.

"Lucia!" He jumped back, startled. "You know, I don't think that I'm ever going to get used to you doing that."

"Doing what?" she asked. Lucia appeared as she had on the previous three nights, a beautiful young girl, shining, with a halo of bright light.

"Just popping up in my back yard like that."

"I am sorry Adam. Is there some other way that–"

"No, no, don't worry about it" he said, waving his hand to cut her off. "After all, I only have eight more nights to see you, right?"

"That is correct" she replied.

"And after that, I guess I'll find out firsthand about all this death stuff, huh?" He made the remark humorously, trying to ease his own fear and apprehension.

Lucia raised her eyebrows, and asked "Is this your question?"

"Oh, no I just – well, yes, I mean it's a good one" Adam stammered. "But not tonight's. You asked me to wait until the last night to ask that one and I will. No, I have another question tonight." He walked over to the swing at the edge of the porch, and sat down.

Lucia, who had been standing at the edge of the patio, followed and sat down beside him. "So have you been reading any more books about me?" she asked, a pleasant, almost playful tone to her voice.

"No. I have a couple of more that have some stuff about you, but I spent today alone with Emily. Listen, I didn't mean to bum you out with all that business about how you were killed and all. I'd just never heard of you, then when I read all those horrible things I just... Well, I'm sorry."

"There is nothing to be sorry about, Adam. You did not 'bum me out' as you so interestingly put it." Lucia looked into his eyes and smiled, assuring him that everything was all right.

"I look at you and I see peace. Will I look like you when, well, you know?"

"Is this your question?" she asked again.

"No, no it's not," he said, holding up both palms as if to stop her from answering. "I guess I'd better ask it now before I slip up on tonight's." He looked down at the ground, gently pushing off with his feet to set the swing into a slow, gentle arc. "This one's pretty important to me, Lucia. It's about Emily. Thinking about the Bible stories that I learned in church, I remember that a bunch of fellows asked Jesus about marriage one time. I think that they were trying to trip him up with a trick question that was about an old custom where if an older brother died then his next younger brother would marry his wife. If he died, then the next younger brother would marry the woman, and so forth. So the question was something like, if that happened a number of times, who would the woman be married to in heaven? Jesus told them that there was no marriage in heaven. Well, I guess that kind of makes it a done deal, but that's not enough for me. As much as we've shared here on Earth together, I can't believe that I'll have the same

63

relationship with Emily that I have with the town barber when we all get to heaven. See my point?"

Lucia was nodding her head. "Ah, I understand what you are asking. A very good question, with a good example. But you have to be careful, Adam. The Bible is a powerful book, and says many things to many people. Most people think of it as a set of words carved in a granite stone, but it is not. It is instead like water in a vessel. Ever-flowing. Make no mistake. The words all serve God's glory and his purpose. It is how He talks to you and gives you wisdom. A sentence might help you in one very special way that you need, but He could use the same sentence to help someone else with a completely different need. It is unfortunate, but wars have been started over the way one man or another interpreted God's word."

"Right; I get that," Adam said, listening intently.

"Good. All that said, you have to understand what the Master meant there. Certainly he meant that there was no marriage in heaven, but he was also responding to a group of men who were trying to deceive him with their intentions. They had no concern on the presence or absence of marriage in heaven. They merely wanted to give him a question that he would not be able to answer."

"I'm not sure that I'm getting your point, Lucia. I understand what you're saying and all, but how does that relate to my question?"

"The way it relates is this: you gave as an example of your question a single passage from the Bible. I am merely explaining that there is more to the topic of you and your wife and your relationship in heaven than is contained in that single sentence. The two of you will not be married, but you will have a special relationship. You will cherish the bond that you had together on earth, but you will each be far beyond your current existence... in a way that you cannot possibly understand now." She paused, thinking of a clearer explanation for him. "You had best friends in your childhood, correct?"

"Of course" he agreed.

"And you have a larger set of friends now. Some that you have met recently, and probably a few from your childhood years."

"Sure."

"At that time in your childhood, your best friend was just that. At the time, it was probably hard to imagine that a relationship in your life could ever be closer."

"I guess so, why?"

"Because at the time, you could not comprehend the idea of a wife and how close the two of you could be. And those childhood best friends that you still know are closer in some ways than those people that you have met at your job. You can still reminisce about your childhood memories together. But you now know that the relationship that you once had, as good as it was, has been replaced by other more advanced relationships such as your spouse."

"I think I see. So we will still know each other, and know how special we were together, but our new existence will be so much more magnificent that the concept of marriage won't apply."

"You do see," she said, and smiled to comfort him. "I know that this answer does not completely satisfy you, but there are many things that you just have to accept on faith. I can do my best to explain it, but you will have to look to God for the peace to understand it in your heart."

"Okay..." Adam said, staring away in thought. As an afterthought, he added "but what about the religions that teach that husband and wife will be together in Heaven?"

Lucia smiled again. "How do you explain the woman married to all those brothers?"

"Ah," he said, satisfied with that answer. "Listen Lucia, I think I just need to be alone out here for a while. Do you mind if I asked you to–"

"Not at all" she said, answering before he could finish his request. "Besides, you won't really be alone. You never are. Look to God to help settle your questions and fears, Adam." She stood, and began to walk away.

Adam watched until she was but a point of light in the far distance in the woods beyond the house, then heaved a heavy sigh and stared out into the cold, evening sky.

The Fifth Day

Sunday, December 17th

The buzzing of the alarm broke the silence of the morning. Emily opened her eyes. Slowly, they adjusted to the light creeping into the room.

"Adam?" she said groggily.

"Ummmhhh," he mumbled.

"Adam, wake up. The alarm's going off." Emily raised herself up on her elbows, peering over her husband at the clock.

"Alarm" he replied, still veiled in sleep.

"No kidding, Adam, come on. I have to go to the store today. Billy can't open. He took his family to his cousin's wedding down in Bryan." She gently shook his sleeping form, then reached over him and clicked off the alarm.

"What time is it?" he asked, slowly starting to stir.

"Nine. Get up – Gerry and Paula should bring Amy by sometime this afternoon, and the house is in bad need of being picked up. You were certainly a party to messing it up – can you use your day off to get everything back in order?"

"That'll work. But on your way out, hang a sign on the door that says 'knock loud to wake Adam'." He pulled the covers up around him, turned over and buried back into the pillow.

"Funny, mister. Let's go. Up!" she said, lovingly shaking his shoulder. "I'm jumping in the shower, then I'm out of here."

* * * * *

Thirty minutes later Emily dashed out of the door, munching on a piece of bread that Adam had toasted for her.

He looked around the kitchen and thought back to the time a decade ago when he and Emily had spent weeks drawing and re-drawing the plans for the house. Although it wasn't a palatial estate, it was the perfect home, and one that they planned on spending the rest of their lives in.

Adam sighed, and said aloud, "Which in my case, won't be a problem." He pulled out a chair from the table in their breakfast nook and sat down, resting his elbows on the table, his face in his hands.

"God," he said, "Why in the world are you doing this to me? I don't understand." His eyes welled up with tears, and he said, "You gave me the perfect life, but instead of simply snatching it away from me, you sent someone in advance to tell me that you were going to take it away. It's like you want to torture me."

He leaned back in the chair, took a deep breath, and continued. "Look, I know that I'm all over the map with this. When I talk to Lucia, I feel comforted that everything is going to be fine. In the middle of the day when I'm alone, I feel like crap – I'm scared to death, I'm worried about what's going to happen to me, and I'm frightened for my family." After a pause, he yelled, "What the hell are you doing to me?"

The room was silent, and he finally put his face back into his hands. He cried until there seemed to be no tears left. Finally, he continued. "Look, I'm sorry, I shouldn't be yelling. I just – well, I mean if it's possible – could we find some way where I don't have to die right now? Maybe even give me another few years? God, I promise you with all my heart that I'll be good. I'll go to church, I'll make sure and tithe, I'll even sing in the choir. You just can't let me die right now!"

Again, there was nothing but silence throughout the house. When he scooted the chair back to stand up, it seemed to echo off the walls. Adam stood, and finally said, "Guess that's a no, then." He wished that the evening were here already. The only thing that seemed to offset the prospect of his impending death – his only link to God – was Lucia.

* * * * *

Adam glanced back at the clock – 12:25 AM. He stepped out onto the porch, looking around in the darkness for a hint of her presence. "Lucia?" he asked cautiously, determined that she would not startle him tonight.

"I am here, Adam."

"Where?" he asked, seeing no trace of the brilliant light that usually accompanied her.

"Here" the voice said, off to his right side.

As Adam was turning his head, the light grew until he was looking at the form of the young girl once again. "That's a little better."

"I do try. So how are you this evening, Adam?" she said.

Adam marveled at her. When she spoke, every word was sincere. "I'm fine. A little worried, but fine."

"Worried about?"

"What else?" he asked in a matter-of-fact tone. "I don't know, Lucia, it's weird. One moment I'm as happy and content as ever. I feel like I'm living life to the fullest, loving my family, thinking about friends, making the most of every minute. The next moment, though, it hits me that I have a little over a week to live."

She stood serene and still, a few feet away from the patio. "So how do you feel about dying?" she asked.

"Different. At least when I'm with you, I have to say that you've alleviated some of the base fears that I had, but I'm not sure that I've fully digested all the information that you've given me," he said, still confused by his conflicting feelings.

"You are besieged with a lot, Adam. Many people take a lifetime to form opinions on what awaits them at their mortal end. For humans, it is a never-ceasing search for the truth." She looked deeply into his eyes. "You have been given many truths, Adam. It is almost more than the human mind can grasp – actually relating these truths to the anticipation of death, that is."

"Yeah, I suppose" he relented.

"Be patient, and don't force yourself to categorize any feelings at all. Let God work with them in your mind and soul, and trust me, you will find peace."

He shook his head. "You know, Lucia, I'm really not sure."

"Because of your prayer today?"

Adam looked quickly to her. "How'd you know about that?" He paused, and then added, "Were you listening in?"

"I am afraid that I do not have the privilege of hearing prayers to God. No, instead, He told me about it." She raised her chin a bit, and smiled. "He was delighted that you talked to Him – as you said once before, it has been a while. But we should get to your question about death for this evening. Have you decided what it will be?"

He turned and took a few steps across the patio, gazing out into the night sky. "Sure, I guess it had been a while since I've prayed, but after seeing you these last few nights I expected something..." he searched for the words. "I don't know, something more real. Instead, it wasn't a big deal at all; I was supposed to be sitting there talking to God. Instead, I felt like I was in the room all alone, talking to the furniture." He shrugged. "I mean, how do you know that God is listening?"

Her gaze never wavering, Lucia said, "God is always listening. Always. To everything. But time passes quickly this evening – what is your question for me tonight?"

After thinking about that for a moment, Adam said, "Hold on a sec. So He heard me asking about saving me from dying?"

Lucia took a step back, shaking her head from side to side. "Adam, you just don't understand. God is the architect of all that is, all that has been, and all that will ever be. He created the universe in all its glory, but also the tiny ant bed at the corner of your yard. He sees all, knows all, is all." She sighed. "Believe me, He hears you. But that is not a question that–"

Adam quickly put up his index finger. "Ah, but it is. On the first night, you told me that I could not ask about the exact time or circumstance of my death until our last night together. Tonight, I'm simply asking why God wouldn't respond to my plea to give me just a little longer." Adam crossed his arms. "It's a fair question about death. So, why didn't He answer?"

Lucia was silent for a moment, turned away, and walked to the edge of the patio. After a long pause, she turned and walked back. "You are correct – it is a fair question. Why do you think that He did not answer you?"

"Because of what I asked. I just wanted a little more time." Adam stopped to compose himself. "If He had answered my prayer, you wouldn't be here – there would be no need for it."

She smiled knowingly. "Because you wouldn't be dying if he did?"

"Exactly!" Adam said, waving his hands for emphasis.

"You want to talk to God as you do to me – to hear His voice, to receive direct answers to your queries. Is that what I am to understand?"

Adam was silent for a moment, and said, "Well, it would certainly make everything more clear."

She reached out and placed her hand on his shoulder. When she did, it felt warm, and his entire body seemed to tingle and relax. "You must understand, Adam, that your human mind cannot comprehend God, much less see him or hear his spoken voice – I do not want to be dramatic, but being in his divine presence, well, the experience would tear your fragile body apart." She removed her hand, and then suddenly stopped. "Wait; we are missing someone tonight."

For a moment Adam was confused, and then he turned and knocked on the sliding glass door leading into the house. From beside it, Elvis eased out of the doggie door, shaking his head, and looking around.

"Forgive me," Lucia said, and reached down to scratch the dog's head. "But he gives me such pleasure. How old is this wonderful hound?"

"Nine. Starting to get up to his golden years." Adam couldn't help but smile when talking about Elvis. "I worry about him getting old; we could only have him another three or four years. I mean, Emily could."

"Humans obsess on age." She stood back up, and looked Adam in the eye. "In a hospital a half-hour away there is a man born only two weeks later than you, and tonight he will pass from a failure of his heart. One floor down, a ninety-eight-year-old man will die in about fifteen minutes from pneumonia. On the same floor, a nine-year-old boy will pass from injuries of a terrible accident. Do you not understand? Humans are fragile, and every day is a gift. You could be standing here with an embolism in your brain that will kill you tomorrow, yet never showed a single symptom." She turned and walked halfway across the yard, and then looked back. "Age is a false sense of security for the young, and nothing more." As Elvis trotted across the yard toward her, she said, "But for what it is worth, I think that he has many years left."

"Unlike me," Adam said flatly.

She paused, and then said, "Adam, do you think your prayer that unique? A thousand people pray the same thing to God a thousand times a day. He hears each and every one. Even Christ prayed the same thing in the Garden of Gethsemane, when he said, 'Father, if you are willing, please take this cup from me'."

"I notice that it didn't work out too well for him, either," Adam said flatly.

"The important thing to note is what Christ added. He also said, 'But not my will, but yours, be done'. Even knowing how terrible the experience would be, he turned it completely over to God."

It was Adam's turn to stop and reflect. "And you think that's what I should do about this whole death thing, even though it seems that he isn't answering my prayers?"

Lucia smiled. "Adam, you should turn everything over to God. But you should keep talking to him – he loves hearing from you, especially since it has been quite a while."

Adam shook his head. "Well, I prayed a lot as a kid. 'Now I lay me down to sleep' when I was going to bed, 'God is great, God is good, let us thank Him for this food' at the table, but nothing cosmic."

Her smile turned into a downright grin. "But God loves the prayers of children – you would be surprised how special those are to Him."

"Yeah, but I'm an adult now. And today felt weird."

"It probably felt 'weird', Adam, because you haven't done it in a while. I cannot say it strongly enough: God loves hearing from you. And remember what the Bible says: pray without ceasing. He really likes that." With that, she took a few steps away, before being interrupted by Adam.

"So I should just sit at home and pray all day?" he asked.

Once again she smiled and shook her head. "No, of course not. If you had been doing that, you couldn't have prospered at the company where you work, and you would have been dismissed for attendance issues. Emily would be angry with you, and your paycheck would not have been around to help feed Amy, so your life would have been a disaster."

"Okay," he shrugged. "I give. What does that mean?"

"I feel that you are missing the point. To 'pray without ceasing' does not mean to engage in formal prayer..." she shook her head, frustrated. Turning around, she looked into the night for a moment, and then finally turned back. "Tell me about dinnertime at your house," she said.

"Well," Adam said, "it's kind of an important time to my family. Emily and I pitch in on getting the meal ready, and once we put it on the table, we start talking about our day. We ask Amy what she did during the day, what she worked on in class, and even what the cafeteria served for lunch. Emily then tells us about her day at the store, and I wind things up with the most boring part, my life at the office." After a moment he added, "It's really a bonding time for the family, though."

"Yes," Lucia said definitively, "and that is what God wants from you. He wants to hear about your day as you go through it – the things that you like, dislike, fear, and celebrate, all are important to him as your Heavenly Father, just as you care about Amy. He wants to hear you say, 'Lord, thank you for this parking space,' or 'Father, I am so worried about this project at work,' or 'Please let me keep this thing in perspective'. Talk to him all day, about everything – believe me, he wants to hear from you just like you want to hear from your daughter Amy! Just keep an open dialogue. He hears you, and is listening and reacting to each and every one of your prayers."

"Except about giving me a little more time?"

Lucia began to walk away. "No, even that one. But even though He heard you, He may not be answering in a way that you expect." Starting to skate on the frosty grass, passing through the fence, he heard her call, "But please, Adam, do not stop talking to Him..."

The Sixth Day

It was a cold morning, even though the sun was up and there wasn't a cloud in the sky. Benjamin Robertson was in his equipment shed, which although covered by a corrugated tin roof, was open on all sides to allow balers, rakers, mowers and other equipment to be simply pulled in from any direction and parked.

Ben had spent the morning greasing his round-baler. A hay baler shared the same requirements of any piece of machinery – a drop of oil here, a squirt of grease here, and a bit of tenderness when using it. During the summer he worked the equipment until it was about to fall apart, but the fall and winter months gave him time to pamper them: spray on paint to prevent rusting, repair any damage from the working season, and perform any general upkeep.

He was removing the grease gun from the last port when he heard the gravel crunching under someone's footsteps. He craned his neck from under the machine, only to see his old high school nemesis approaching.

"Hey, Ben" Adam said cautiously, raising his hand in greeting.

"Adam." The reply was flat, without emotion. "Never expected to see you set foot on my property." As he spoke, he wriggled out from under the monstrous baler. He wiped the grease from his hands with a rag that he carried in his back pocket for that express purpose. "Can't say that I'm all that excited about it, either."

"I figured you wouldn't be. But it's high time that I did. There's been bad blood between us for way too many years." He paused for a minute, and then added, "And for my part in it, well, today I've come to say that I'm sorry."

Ben slowly shook his head from side to side. "Not interested."

"Aw, hell, Ben, we have to let all that go – it was decades ago!" Adam said.

It was a full minute before Ben spoke. "Look, you son-of-a-bitch, you ruined my life. When you crossed over into my territory to catch that ball–"

Adam winced. "For crying out loud, Ben, don't you understand that you were playing too close to the foul line, and there's no way that you could have made it over to catch that pop-up? It was a high school baseball game, and nothing more! All I did was grab it to put the batter out – and if I hadn't, he would have had a base hit, and they could have gone on to win the game."

"I think I could've got it," Ben said flatly. "But even if I couldn't, I would have grabbed it on a bounce and thrown him out at first." He stood there staring at Adam. "But no, you snagged it and got all the credit for winning the game. The scouts were in the stands and gave you all the scholarships, and while you were away having one big party at college, I was taking over my daddy's land. My hands were bleeding from work, while you were tapping kegs of beer every week." After a moment, he spat on the ground.

Taking a deep breath, holding it, and slowly exhaling, Adam finally said, "Ben, you're full of crap. You couldn't have caught the ball, and I doubt that you could have thrown it to first base in time for an out. But who cares? That was back in high school during our senior year. It happened years ago, for cryin' out loud!"

"Funny," Ben said, "I remember it like it was yesterday."

"Well, maybe you do, but I don't." Adam's eyes narrowed. "And as far as all those scholarships, I applied for over twenty of them, and only got four – but it was enough to help me go to college. If I remember what you said back then, you applied for three and didn't get any. That's not my fault, that's just the law of averages at work. You should have gone at it harder." After a moment's pause, he added, "And only one of those scholarships that I got was for sports, so catching that fly ball didn't do anything for me that night."

"Really? Well now who's full of crap..." Ben said through clenched teeth. He balled his fists.

Adam stood silently for a minute. "Okay, I just had to try. I'd hate to get hit by an eighteen-wheeler out on the highway, and have to check out of this life holding a grudge. So let me just say again..." he stared at Ben, and with genuine compassion, said, "I am truly sorry that it ever happened. If I had it to do over again, I'd let that ball go. But I can't." He turned and began to walk away. "It doesn't have to be like this, Ben. It really doesn't."

Ben took a step forward. "Yeah, well screw you. Don't you ever come back on my property. Hear me?" He poked an index finger toward Adam for emphasis.

Adam walked a few steps further, then stopped and turned around. "The funny thing is, you've taught me a lesson today, Ben."

Eyes narrowed, Ben said, "What do you mean?"

"Remember back in High School when Mrs. Pierce made us read *Moby Dick*? We had to memorize passages and stand up and recite them in front of the class."

"Stupid, boring book," Ben said flatly.

Adam smiled. "Yeah, I thought so, too. But I've always been able to recite the things that I memorized back in school. I just didn't understand them. But you know, thanks to you, I at least understand one thing." He looked out across the pastures for a moment, closed his eyes, and then quoted from memory, "And he piled upon the whale's white hump the sum of all the rage and hate felt by his whole race. If his chest had been a cannon, he would have shot his heart upon it..."

Ben was silent for a moment. His brow furled, and he finally said, "You must have lost your freakin' mind. What the hell are you talking about?"

"*Moby Dick*. It's a line from *Moby Dick*," Adam said. "And Ben, it's what you're doing. Whatever problems you've had in your life, you're blaming them on me and that one baseball catch, much like old Ahab turned all his rage onto the great white whale. Wow, I'd never understood the book before... but I certainly do now." He laughed to himself. "Wow. Wish I had time to re-read it."

After several moments of silence, Ben said, "Look, you're acting crazy. Just get your ass off my property, and I mean right this second, or I'm going to call the sheriff."

Adam nodded. "Done. But I want you to know something. From this moment forward, whenever I see you in town, I'm going to speak to you like you are my best friend. I'll wave at you every time I pass you on the road, and I'm going to think nothing but good thoughts about you." He started to turn and leave, but paused. "Whatever bad feelings are between us, they're strictly yours now, Ben. You own them."

The man just stared at him, then turned his head and spat onto the ground. Adam walked back down the gravel drive toward his car, feeling lighter with each step.

* * * * *

At midnight, Adam opened the sliding door and stepped out onto the patio. Elvis followed closely behind.

"Lucia?" he asked.

The darkness of the night was cut by a bright flash, and in only an instant the girl was standing out on the grass.

"Good evening, Adam," she said with a nod and a smile.

"You know, it is a good one. It's been a very good day, in fact."

"So I have heard." Elvis trotted over to her, and Lucia bent down to rub his head, tussling his floppy ears in the process. "It is a wonderful thing that you did."

Adam shrugged his shoulders. "I'm not so sure. It didn't turn out all that well."

"Really?" She crossed her arms, and cocked her head to one side. "And how have you determined that?"

"Well, Ben is as angry and stubborn as ever." After a moment he added, "I was hoping to patch things up."

Lucia took a step toward him. "But don't you see? You cannot control his feelings, any more that he can control yours. Stop and think – how did you feel about him yesterday?"

Adam searched inside himself for the right answer. "I don't know. It's complicated. I mean, I didn't hate him or anything, but I didn't like him, either. When I'd come home from college I'd hear that he'd been talking bad about me to our friends, and every time we ran across each other we had nothing but harsh words. I guess all that made me angry."

Her eyes locked on his, and once again, it was as if she was looking into his very soul. "Angry at him, or at yourself?"

81

The question made Adam pause. "Well, at him, of course…"

"Are you sure?"

Adam stood silently for a full minute, and then walked over to a wooden chair and sat down. "Wow."

"Wow?" Lucia said, smiling again. "Please explain."

After another pause, Adam said, "You know, this time yesterday I would have sworn that I was mad at him. But after kind of airing things out today, it feels like a lot of anger is gone – different kinds, in different directions. Maybe some at Ben, and some, I guess, at me."

She nodded.

"You know, when I left him today I felt like a huge weight had been lifted off my shoulders…"

"And so it had," Lucia interjected.

"But I also felt an incredible sadness for Ben, who's still carrying that burden around. I mean, even right this moment."

She stood there for a moment in silence, before saying, "Your friend's burden is his own to bear. He willingly continues to do so."

Adam smiled. "Yeah, well, I'm going to do something about that. Ben is going to become my pet project. When I see him on the street I'm going to smile and wish him the most heart-felt greeting that he's ever had – and I'll continue to do so. I don't care if I only have a few days left, my goal for as long as I'm still breathing is to try to break through that icy-exterior of his, and to become his friend again."

Lucia nodded. "A noble endeavor."

"Thanks. I really believe so." Adam walked out to the edge of the patio, and just stared at the stars for a moment. "Yep, that's what I'm going to do." He turned and smiled. "I'm going to be all right, I think," he said. "My question tonight is about this very kind of thing."

Lucia nodded her head once, "Please, proceed."

"We talked about the burden that I felt lifted as I was leaving Ben's, but what would have happened if hadn't gone over there before, well, before *it* happens – my death, I mean. Before talking to him I had no idea that weight was even there. If I hadn't gotten rid of it, would I have taken it with me after death?" He paused for a moment, and then added, "I guess that sounds kind of silly when I hear it said out loud, but it's something that I've been thinking about all day."

"There is nothing foolish about your question, Adam." She looked away, and then back into his eyes with a smile. "In fact, what I am going to tell you is profound, and to mortals who would try to understand it, borders on the miraculous."

Adam crossed his arms and his eyes narrowed. "Okay, you've certainly got my attention now. I'm all ears – what is this miracle answer?"

"It is simply this: negative human feelings and emotions have no place in heaven... but they can be all-powerful on earth. They can hold complete dominion over a person." She stepped forward, and put her hand on his shoulder. He felt a warm tingle go through it as she looked into his eyes. "It seems like such a simple concept, but understanding this one thing can prevent or even heal disease, bring untold prosperity, and allow one's life to be filled with love. It has that kind of power." She stepped back, and shook her head. "This will be difficult to explain in such a short time..."

It was a full minute before she spoke again. "Heaven is a perfect place, Adam. There is no sorrow, no pain, no worry, no stress. Some of it is because of the nature of the place – after all, you have no physical needs. You won't get hungry, you'll never be cold, there will be no bills or financial worries, and the weak physical body that you have now will no longer restrict you."

Lucia walked slowly to the edge of the patio, with Elvis plodding along after her, and she finally turned around to face

Adam. "It's more than that, however. You will see and comprehend things with a completely different perspective. Everything that is so crucial and imperative now will seem like a childish folly. You will understand everything, and you will walk with God."

Adam slowly nodded his head. "Sounds incredible. Sounds – well, perfect."

"Perfection is what God is all about. But that is only half of my answer to you tonight." Lucia sighed. "All those things that are so blissfully absent in heaven, are actually powerful forces here on Earth. The human body is so fragile to begin with, but to add stress, worry, and hate can tear down its defenses and open the door to many problems."

"Yeah, I've always heard that stress kills," Adam agreed.

"This is more than just a saying." Lucia's face had become very serious. "Most people carry deeply-rooted negative feelings around with them – these feelings become so much a part of their lives that they don't even realize they're there. The negativity, for the most part unfelt and unseen, begins to slowly eat away at them like a cancer. When it eventually comes out – which it always does – it does so as disease, hatred, and even self-destruction of the person."

Adam smiled. "So all you have to do is chill out, and your life will be a lot better?"

"Oh, if only it was that easy. Letting go of negative feelings and purging them from your mind and body is something that humans simply are not equipped to do." She took a few steps, shaking her head. "No, it is a constant battle to keep the negative out of your mind. It is not something that you decide to do, and it is done. You must focus on the positive – love, gratitude, and forgiveness."

"I can do that," Adam said, nodding.

Lucia stood there, looking at him. A sad smile slowly crossed her face. "No, Adam, I fear that you cannot. Nor could any human."

"Lucia, do you realize what I've been through the last few days? Thanks to you, I've gotten a glimpse into the other side – into your realm! Of course I can!"

She shook her head. "It is God's realm, not mine, and your experiences are thanks to Him, not me. I am merely His messenger. But you are but a man, and while your spirit is shining and bright, you are still only a mortal in this world. If Ben strikes out at you by spreading bad words about your wife or your daughter, your anger would come back ten-fold, no matter how much you would wish it away."

He shrugged. "Okay, so you're saying that there's no hope – that I might as well not even try to be a good person?"

"Not at all, Adam. Quite the opposite." She turned and walked across the patio, stared into the night sky, and finally faced him again. "Look up. Do you see the moon, reflecting light down around us?"

"Of course; I love looking up at it at night. There's something mysteriously beautiful about it." His voice trailed off as he gazed up at the celestial body.

"Do you know that on its surface, there is a flag of your nation standing in the soil?"

Adam chuckled. "Well, I haven't seen it in person, but I've certainly seen pictures."

"It is there; believe me. But do you know how difficult it was to place there?"

He looked over to her. "You mean – you've seen it? You've been there?"

Lucia closed her eyes; "Stay with me, Adam." She began to slowly pace. "The reason that I talk about it at all is this: you have no idea of the complications that it took to make the placement of that flag happen. It took millions of human dollars, the careers of many people, even the sacrifice of several lives before man could reach the moon."

"Sure, I've seen the documentaries, I know the history," Adam said.

"Then you should be aware that if you were to casually say, 'I will go to the moon' it would be a foolish statement – it would be far beyond the abilities of a singular human to accomplish such a feat." Lucia paused for a moment. "But thanks to a massive effort, a man did walk on the moon. It is the same when you say that you will practice love, gratitude and forgiveness. You could easier reach the moon on your own than to embrace these emotions and purge your heart of all negativity. But just as the astronauts had a massive effort behind them, you have the awesome power of God at your disposal. You have but to ask, believe, and go forward in faith… but that can be extraordinarily difficult. The weakness is not in God's gifts, but in man's ability to receive and maintain them."

Adam took a deep breath. "But I can at least try, right?"

Lucia smiled. "God loves to see his children seeking His ways. It pleases Him immensely, and He blesses those who do so." With that, she turned and began to walk away. "You are in a good place at the moment, Adam, but keep this in mind… you will stumble, you will fall, you will fail." She turned and took a few more steps, before pausing again. "Tell me, Adam, would you burn with hatred for your basset hound if he were to have an accident and – what's the word – 'pee' in the house?"

"Of course not," he said. "It doesn't happen often, but there are rare occasions. We just point it out to him and clean it up. I couldn't be angry with Elvis, and certainly couldn't hate him – he's part of our family, but after all, he's just a dog."

"And you're just a human. But to God, you're much more important than a mere pet – you're His child, His creation, and

He loves you in ways that are truly beyond your understanding. He knows and cherishes everything about you."

"So... what does that mean for me?"

"Talk to Him. Without ceasing, like He asked. And the worse you feel, the more anger, the more hatred, talk to Him even more. Yell at Him as you did yesterday; believe me, He can take it. He can carry the burdens when you can't even begin to." After a pause, she said, "And with that, I will take my leave for the evening."

Adam looking nervously away, "There's something else, though; something different. I'm worried as to whether or not I should be telling all this to Emily... I mean, telling her about you – about... what's coming."

Lucia was silent for a moment, and then said "Do as your heart leads, Adam, but consider this. There is no easy way to explain my presence here. It was hard for you to accept, even as I was standing before you. If you tell her your perspective of everything that is happening in your life, it might only frighten or confuse her."

Adam thought about it for a few moments, and then said, "You're probably right. I may tell her, but I'll wait until I can sort more of this out."

"A wise decision, I would think," Lucia said. She walked away, fading into the night.

The Seventh Day

Tuesday, December 19th

The ringing of the phone woke Adam. He turned over and looked at the clock, which showed nine-thirty; clearly Emily had turned off the alarm to let him sleep in. He stretched and yawned, then contemplated turning back over for another half hour. After only a moment, he realized that every passing moment was precious, and swung his legs over the side of the bed.

Emily came dashing into the room, and he could immediately see that something was terribly wrong. She had a blank expression, and it was if she was trying to speak, but nothing was coming out.

"You okay, babe?" he said, standing up and stepping over to her. He put his arm around her shoulder. "What is it?"

"It–it's…" She put her hands up to her face, and then finally pulled them away. "I just got a call from Billy." Emily shook her head slowly from side to side, as if denying her thoughts. "Mary Robertson was leaving for work this morning; Ben had already gone out to start his day. As she was backing out of the driveway, she saw him lying on the ground near their

89

farm shed. She ran over to him, but it was too late – he was gone."

Adam took a step back, and sat down onto the bed. "Gone… you mean, dead?"

She shook her head up and down slowly.

"Oh my God… I just saw him yesterday…"

"You did?" Emily asked, confused. "But you two haven't spoken for years. What in the world?"

He shook his head. "I don't know, I was just kind of hoping to patch things up, but it didn't go like I'd planned." Adam sat there for a moment. "He was as angry as ever – it's like hate was radiating off of him. Later on, I was hoping that maybe I could break through one of these days… or, at least start trying for now. I knew that we'd probably never be best friends, but I wanted to get rid of the bad blood between us."

She ran her hand through her red hair, pulling it off of her face. "They think that it must have been a heart attack." Emily looked over to her husband. "But he was your age! How could someone that young…"

Adam thought back to Lucia's words from a few nights ago, and softly said, "No one gets any guarantees."

"I know but…" She wiped a tear from her eye. "C'mon, get dressed. Let's go see Mary; maybe there's something we can do." Turning and walking to the closet, she added, "Poor Mary; she's got to be losing her mind right now."

The realization hit him like a freight train. If Lucia was correct, than how long would it be – a week at the most – until he was gone? People would be saying "Poor Emily" and rushing to see what they could do to help her and Amy. They'd be remembering him, pitying his wife, and after only a few days life would go on. Emily would start healing from the loss, and after only a year or two Amy would probably be struggling to even remember him. It was Adam's turn to cry, as tears fell from his face to the bedcover.

When Emily saw him, she rushed over and put her arms around her husband. "It's okay, dear, it's okay." Holding him tightly, she said, "I never would have thought that you'd have such an emotional reaction – I didn't think that you two were connected at all!"

Adam pulled away and wiped his tears. "I'll be fine. Let's get ready and go see Mary."

* * * * *

The kitchen of the Robertson home was already filling with food. Adam shook his head – it was a small-town tradition, bringing covered dishes to a home that had experienced the loss of a loved one. In some ways it made sense – family members would be coming in for the funeral, and it spared the grieving loved ones from having to prepare meals. It was probably just as much for the people who brought the food, however. What else could they possibly offer, and it did let them feel like they were doing something to help out.

As he surveyed the dishes on the counter, he mentally checked off each of the standards: fried chicken, green bean casserole, banana pudding... everything seemed to be there.

"Adam–" Emily's voice interrupted his culinary inventory. "Mary's asking to see you."

He nodded and followed his wife into the family room, where Mary Robertson sat in a rocking chair. Her eyes were red and swollen, and her hair was pulled haphazardly back into a ponytail. She looked rough, but one could expect little more on such an occasion.

"Mary," he said, taking her hands. "I'm so very sorry for your loss. Ben was much too young for something so terrible to happen to him. Please, if there's anything at all that we can do, you only have to pick up the phone."

The young widow smiled. "You already did it, Adam, and I can't thank you enough."

Confused, Adam said, "Okay, but what are you talking about?"

"You came to see Ben yesterday. I don't know what the two of you talked about, but it was all that he could go on about last night. He was angry with you, and paced all over this room while he was cursing you, but I've been married to that man for over ten years – I could tell that something was different. I know that you somehow found a chink in my husband's armor yesterday, and opened a door. He just wasn't able to admit it. Not yet." She half-laughed, half-sobbed. "You touched him, and for that, I sincerely thank you."

"Oh, Mary." He fought back tears. "Ben and I wasted so much time with petty differences. I only wish that I could have reached out to him sooner. But, who knew…" His voice trailed off; he had no idea what to say.

She gently kissed the back of his hand that she was still holding. "God bless you and Emily. Please, please, enjoy your life together. I never dreamed that ours could end so abruptly, so cherish every single moment."

It was too much for Adam; Lucia's first-night message meant that his clock was ticking, and he knew that he had precious few days left with Emily. Tears flowed, and he simply smiled, gripped her hands, and walked out of the room. He felt guilty that the tears were not for Ben or Mary, but for himself and his wife.

* * * * *

"God damn it, Lucia, where are you?" he hissed through clenched teeth. Adam paced violently back and forth across the patio, as he'd been doing for the past ten minutes.

A light exploded behind him, and he turned around to see her standing at the far edge of the patio. Elvis was on her immediately, jumping up and putting his front paws on her legs. She smiled as she petted him. "At least someone is happy to see me."

Adam turned to face her, indignant. "What kind of game are you playing with my life? I told you last night that I was going to reach out to Ben with whatever time I had left." He fought back tears, and with a raised voice said, "You could have told me that he was going to die!"

She shrugged her shoulders. "But I had no idea. How could I?"

Pointing a finger at her, Adam said, "You talk to God – that's what you said. Didn't 'God' give you some kind of clue as to what was happening? After you left last night did you and 'God' sit back and have a good laugh at me wanting to help a former friend that was just a few hours away from a heart attack? Damn it, Lucia, how can I trust you?"

She stood there quietly, and after a moment said, "I was thrilled that you had made such progress, even if it appeared to be only on your end. I had no idea that Ben's death was so imminent. In fact, you probably knew about it before I did."

He took a deep breath. "Okay, fine. That's just great. Here's my question for the evening – why did God take Ben when we were just starting to make progress? Was it to punish him, or me, or both? Mary's on her own now, and they have a son that's the same age of my Amy. Back when things got tough, I heard that he took a mortgage on the farm to bring in some money, and now I don't know how Mary's going to pay it. Was this just God giving me a preview of how He's going to screw over Emily and Amy? This is one hell of a contradiction for a God who supposedly espouses love!" He was almost shouting as he finished.

Lucia turned and walked away, going out to the edge of the fence, and stopping. She looked up to the star-filled sky, then finally turned and walked back to the patio. "Adam, you're looking for someone to blame for Ben's death... and perhaps not for his death, but how you are mapping it onto your own. You would blame God, and you would even blame me. What if I told you that Ben has been experiencing chest pains for a month now, and simply dismissed them? That his arteries had blockage and his body had been giving him signals for some time? What if I told you that had he consulted a doctor, a very simple medical procedure could have kept him alive for many years to come?" Lucia sighed and shook her head. "Adam, Adam... you blame God when you should be blaming Ben himself. He chose to ignore the warning signs – remember, God gives everyone free will, and Ben made his own choices... and chose very poorly. He then paid for those choices."

"Okay," Adam said defiantly, "so forget Ben. Here I am about to die, and I haven't had any warning signs. I'm not ignoring any problems – I even went to the doctor to find out what was wrong with me, and everything's fine! Why is God striking me down, leaving my wife as a widow? Can you explain that?"

Lucia bowed her head for a moment, and finally said, "You've already asked your question for the evening, and I have answered it. It pains me to think that you wasted this evening over anger, but I am bound to follow your wishes." She turned and walked away, but when she reached the fence, she turned back around. "Know that God has a plan that you cannot understand, but He does allow man's free will to factor into it. Ben's death was his own fault, and as to yours, I cannot comment further until the last evening we have together. But know that God loves you deeply – He told me so Himself – and is with you every step of your life, and beyond." She turned, and quickly disappeared into the darkness of the night.

Adam stood there, confused, saddened, and more than a little frightened. He opened the sliding glass door, and quietly crept back to the bedroom, followed by Elvis. The basset was asleep within minutes, but it did not come so easily for Adam.

The Eighth Day

"That was nice," Emily whispered. "I think that the service really helped Mary." She put her arm through Adam's, and pulled him close. "We need to go back and see her."

"Of course. I feel terrible for her; I can't imagine a wife being suddenly left so…" Adam choked on the words, and for a moment, fought back tears. "It's just…"

"It's okay, I'm kind of broken up by this whole thing myself. C'mon," Emily said, and together they weaved through the mass of people in the foyer of the funeral home's chapel. At one end, they found the widow in a circle of family.

"Oh, Mary…" Emily said, and hugged her tightly.

Adam put his arms around them both, and said, "If there's anything – and I mean anything – that we can do, from helping you with any further arrangements, to taking care of relatives that have come into town for the service, please don't hesitate to ask. Really, Mary…"

The woman looked up at them both, her eyes red from crying, and said, "Thank you – I'll be calling on my friends, because I fear that I'll be needing all the help that I can get."

"We'll be here for you," Emily said with another hug. They said their goodbyes, and walked silently through the crowd to the parking lot. Stopping at Adam's truck, Emily said, "Well, I guess I have to get back to work. What's on your agenda?"

"I've made an appointment with the school to go have lunch with Amy. I thought that we'd do the dad-and-daughter thing."

Emily smiled. "That's sweet. I think that she's going to really enjoy it." She kissed him on the cheek. "You're a great dad." As she walked away, she popped him on the rear with her hand. "And a hot one, too!"

Adam couldn't help but notice how beautiful she was, with the huge grin on her face. He gave a quick wave goodbye, and opened the door to his truck.

* * * * *

Adam pulled on the front door to the school and stepped into the wide, glass vestibule. He saw a window at the side slide open, and a familiar face appeared.

"Hi, Adam! We've been expecting you," Maribell Franks, the school receptionist said. "I'll buzz you right in."

There was a clicking noise, and one of the doors leading into the school cracked open. Pulling it, he stepped inside and walked over to the office.

"Come on over and I'll get you checked in." Maribell's bubbly voice continued. She pushed a visitor log and a pen across the counter to him. "Just sign it, put the time, and that you're coming to have lunch with Amy. How's Emily, by the way? Why, I haven't seen her in a month of Sundays."

As Adam scrawled his name, he said, "Oh, she's fine. Had to work at the store today, but it's that time of year."

"Well of course; you tell her 'hi' for me, though. Here, now put this on." She handed a piece of paper the size of a credit card to him; it had his name, the date and time, and the word *Cafeteria* in bold letters at the bottom.

He saw that it was a sticker, so he removed the back and attached it to his shirt above his pocket.

"And that's all we need – you're official now. I'll get someone to walk you to the lunchroom." As she glanced around for an aide, the principal, Nancy Greene emerged from the hallway.

"Hey, Adam! I'll be happy to take you back." She reached out and shook his hand. "I heard that you were coming today." Taking his elbow, she steered him down a hallway. "You know, I wish that more parents would come and have lunch with their kids every now and then. It's a positive experience that is simply invaluable." They'd passed a number of classrooms and another hallway or two, before the principal steered him through a pair of double doors.

It seemed to Adam that school cafeterias hadn't changed in decades, although they seemed somehow smaller. It was probably because he hadn't been in one for a very long time.

The principal took him to a table on the far side of the room, and pulled a chair out for him. "We usually sit our parents over here, as far away from the noise as possible. Just have a seat and Amy will be out shortly. Since you were on today's schedule, I'm sure that her teacher has been notified. Thanks again for visiting – parents are always welcome!"

"Thank you," Adam said, "I really appreciate it." He sat down in a chair that was just a tad too small, and as Ms. Greene walked away, he looked around at the lunch room. Students were just starting to file in and get in the line to be served. He considered how great it would be to go back and be that young and innocent again. It would be wonderful to have no worries about finances, mortgages, growing old, or… or death.

Adam's thoughts were interrupted as he heard a cry of, "Daddy!" Amy was bounding across the cafeteria, grinning, arms outstretched. He grabbed his daughter, picked her up, spun her around once, and then said, "Wow, is this great or what? I can't believe that I've never come to eat lunch with you!"

Still smiling, she said, "Maybe you can come every week!"

He paused for a moment, and said, "Who knows, Amy. If I can, I'd like nothing better than to do just that." He took a deep breath, composing himself, and asked, "Okay, what's the plan?"

"Well," she announced proudly, "kids whose parents are here get to cut in line, so let's go get lunch!"

Adam followed her to the front of the line, and while there was some grumbling among the kids, she stepped in front and defiantly said, "My dad is here!" He nodded apologetically at the children, and then looked to the lady at the cash register. She was swiping Amy's lunch card, which she handed back and then looked to Adam.

"Parents are three bucks," the woman said flatly. "Cash."

It occurred to Adam that lunchroom ladies hadn't changed much over the years, but he smiled politely and pulled three ones from his wallet. The lady took it without expression, and immediately moved on to the student behind him.

In only a few minutes, they had been served a meat patty of some type, complete with markings as if it had been grilled, along with mac-and-cheese, green beans, and a choice of regular or chocolate milk. For dessert there was a brownie, although with the nutrition regulations over the past few years, Adam wondered exactly what might be in it.

They took their seats, Amy sitting across from Adam. "So you do this every day?" he asked.

"No, usually I sit with my friends," Amy said, pointing to a table across the room. Five girls were there, laughing and talking.

"Well, I'm sorry to have taken you away from them today," Adam said, smiling at his daughter.

"It's okay. I'd rather eat lunch with you than them any day." Amy beamed.

"And that's what I like t hear," he said. "By the way, I notice that all your friends are girls. Any guy friends that I should know about?"

Giggling, Amy said, "Daddy, please!"

He stared at her for a moment, a smile on his lips, and finally said, "So there is some boy that you're a little sweet on?"

She rolled her eyes and didn't look at her father for a full minute, and then slyly nodded off to her right. "See the table with the boys over there? There's a boy in the middle with blond hair and a blue shirt on."

Adam nodded. "Yeah, I see him."

"Well, his name is Jeremy, and he's really cute. He's funny, sweet, and all the girls like him, but he doesn't seem to know that I'm even alive."

"Hmmm…" Adam pondered the matter for a moment. "Have you tried talking to him?"

The little girl put down her fork, and sighed. "Of course. But he's only interested in talking about boy stuff."

Adam smiled. "Well, I promise you that it will change as time goes by." He couldn't help but stare at the young boy, and wonder whether he would be dating his daughter in the years to come. For a brief moment, he considered finding the boy later and giving him a serious talking-to, but realized that he would only sound crazy. Instead, he said, "So tell me about your day – how are your classes going?"

Amy launched into a description of how much she loved reading, hated math, and looked forward to recess. Adam laughed with her, gave her advice, and in the course of things, ate the meat patty with the markings as if it had been grilled – which from its taste, clearly it hadn't.

Twenty minutes later, he stood at the table and watched Amy run back into her grade-school world, among friends that she would grow up with, but he would never come to know.

* * * * *

"Aren't you cold?" Adam said to the basset hound, who was lying motionless on the concrete. "I guess you'd move if you were." The night was frigid, and there was still a dusting of snow on the pastures that reflected the moonlight. "Lucia?" Adam said softly. "You out here?"

There was only silence. He looked down at his watch – 12:23 – and looked around in the darkness for her. After a minute went by, Elvis' tail began to thump on the concrete patio. Glancing down at the dog, Adam looked back up to a blinding explosion of light. "Wow, I wish you wouldn't do that!" he said, putting his hand up to shield his eyes.

"My apologies," she said, the brightness waning.

He hesitated, and said, "Well, speaking of apologies, I was way out of line last night. I'm – I'm really sorry."

A pleasant smile crossed her face. "You hurt only yourself, Adam, by wasting the evening with anger."

"Yeah, well... I'll try not to waste any more time. It has become too precious to me." After a moment of silence, he nodded down toward Elvis, who was just getting up and stretching. "I think that he knew you were here before I did."

Lucia reached down and stroked the dog's head and neck. "Perhaps he is paying closer attention than you are." She smiled.

Adam shrugged. "I don't know about that, but I've always heard that small children and animals are more in tune to the supernatural than adults."

"Supernatural..." she said thoughtfully, pausing a moment. "Yes, I like that. I like that very much. I am supernatural!"

Holding up his palms, Adam said, "Hey, no offense, but I don't know how I'd categorize you as anything but that. I mean, a ghost, or saint, or whatever you actually are."

"I am actually Lucia. But what is the supernatural, except those things that are outside of what is 'natural' in your world. The things of heaven – God, his angels, even me, are beyond your natural world." She shook her head. "What a shame. If only you could understand and accept that the 'supernatural' is, in reality, very much a part of your world and around you every day."

"How so?" Adam said, brows furrowed in confusion.

"The angels, for example. They are God's messengers and do his bidding. You see them every day, but just do not know it."

"Okay, tell me then – did I run across any angels today? I mean, I had a fairly simple, straightforward day, and certainly didn't notice any celestial beings." He said with a laugh, but quickly added, "I mean, present company excepted. No offense."

Lucia smiled softly. "None taken." She turned away, took a few steps, and stood silently. When she turned back, she said, "I understand that you visited your daughter at her school today."

"I wanted to see her in that environment. I wanted – I needed – to see her among her friends, and..." his voice trailed off, and tears formed in his eyes. "I don't know how many more days I really have with her."

She nodded. "Of course. A very wise decision. But allow me to ask – do you remember the woman taking the money in the cafeteria?"

"Oh, sure; she was a real sour-puss. Typical cafeteria lady."

Nodding, Lucia said, "And an angel."

Adam was stunned, and stood in silence. Finally he shook his head slowly from side to side, and said, "No way. I mean, she looked like a bitter little woman who was angry at having to spend her life working in a school cafeteria. How could that be an angel?"

Lucia laughed – it was light and melodical. It was a full minute before she could speak. "Oh, Adam, I enjoy talking with you so very much. But do you really believe that angels on earth wear white robes, have huge, glowing wings, and glistening halos? No, no, no..." she said, shaking her head. "You would call them..." she paused, "incognito – in disguise. That's why the Bible says to be kind to strangers, because in doing so, many humans have encountered angels without being aware of it."

Adam was astounded. "An angel at Amy's school... but what was she doing there?"

"You'd have to ask God – I have no idea. I have only been told that the person you saw was angelic," she said pleasantly, as if that was enough of an answer. "But the night wears on, and I am here to answer a question about death. What would you ask tonight?"

He took a deep breath and let it out, as if to dispel all of the confusing talk about angels. "Okay, this is something that I've been thinking about ever since I left Amy's school."

Lucia gave a singular nod of her head. "Please."

"Can I prevent this death? Or, at least postpone it for a while?" he asked hopefully.

"I am sorry, Adam, but you are not permitted to ask about your own death until the last night, and…"

"But wait!" he said, holding up a finger. "This isn't necessarily about my own death – people pray for the sick and dying all the time. Sometimes prayers are answered, sometimes they aren't. I want to know if I can pray for myself and my own deliverance from this."

She looked out into the night, and once again paced away. Elvis followed her, sitting down at her feet when she stopped. There was silence in the cold evening for some time, before Lucia turned to face Adam. "I fear that I will not be able to explain it in a way that you can understand." She sighed. "As I have explained to you before, human bodies are frail – they are merely tissue and blood, and so many things can go wrong in their operation. Just imagine how many different medical conditions there are that can cause a body to stop functioning correctly… to die. Infants die because of defects and diseases in their bodies, as do teenagers, young adults, and old men and women. God never created the earthly body to be perfect – just our heavenly bodies."

"Right, so my body has an imperfection that is going to kill me," Adam said. "Or maybe I'm going to pull out of my driveway and get hit by an oncoming car that will irreparably damage my body. I get that. But my question is, can I pray enough to stop it from happening?"

Lucia looked very sad. "I fear that you will not be satisfied with my answer."

"So it's no, then?"

She shrugged. "It is not no, it is instead that I don't know."

A puzzled expression crossed his face. "Lucia, I don't understand."

"Of course not," she answered. "I told you that you would not be happy with the answer that I gave. But Adam, many people pray for many things. Be assured that God loves His people and wants to bless them in ways that cannot even be measured. But we do not know His ultimate plan and will, so we may ask for things that cannot be granted." She began to step slowly across the patio. "And sometimes, the human faith in God's ultimate power is simply not there. I do not know the true measure of your faith, Adam, only God does. Nor do I know God's plans, so I therefore cannot answer your question, other than to say that yes, it is possible, but there are many other factors to consider."

"Lucia," he said cautiously, "how in the world could I doubt God's power. I mean, I'm talking to you right here in my backyard! You're real, God's real, how could anyone have more faith than I do right now? I know that God has the power to do anything!"

"Then I will leave you to contemplate your faith," Lucia said, and began to walk away. "I know that I have not satisfied you with an answer this evening, but perhaps you have more things to think about."

"But Lucia, in the Bible it says that if I have just a little faith, God can move mountains for me!" he called after her. "Why won't He prevent my death?"

Lucia stopped and spun around. She pointed to one of the metal posts supporting the chain-link fence that surrounded the back yard. "Adam – command that fence-post to move one foot out," she said sternly.

"Wh-what? Why would I try to…"

"Adam!" she interrupted. "Command the fence-post. Now!" After a moment, she added, "Do it!"

He threw up his hands in frustration, then bowed his head, and began, "Almighty God, I would ask you to show your power by…"

"No!" Lucia said harshly. "YOU command it. YOU tell the fence post to move."

Adam shook his head, frustrated, and then pointed his hand at the post. "I order you to move!" he said, feeling more than a little silly.

They stood in silence for a moment, until Lucia observed, "It has not moved."

"Of course not!" Adam said loudly. "It's a fence-post! An inanimate object! It CAN'T move!"

Lucia turned and continued to walk away. She passed through the fence, and just before she disappeared into the night, she said, "Be more attentive when you read the Bible, Adam. What Christ literally said was that if you have the faith of a mustard seed – the smallest seed imaginable, the size of the head of a pin – that you could say to a mountain, 'Move from here to there!' and the mountain will move at your word. By itself, even though it is an inanimate object. A huge mountain, not just a small fence-post. He has given you and all humans that power. He says that nothing – NOTHING – will be impossible to you. But you first must have the smallest, most miniscule amount of faith to claim that power. And that is where humans falter. So can you pray for your death not to come? I might ask you if you could command your death not to come."

"Well, since I've never heard of a man moving a mountain, I assume that this power isn't something that is really available to humans." Adam knew that he sounded frustrated, but wasn't sure at who, or why.

"Really? The disciples performed miracles on Earth, and they did so with the power that God gave to them. The same power that He makes available to all humans. The problem is not with Him, but with human beings themselves." After another step, she added, "You are correct, however; no man has ever moved a mountain with his words." She continued to walk. "But if one realized that God had given him that power, and had the faith to use it, perhaps he would not feel the need to waste it on such trivial tasks." She vanished into the darkness, but Adam stood there staring at the fence-post for a very long time.

The Ninth Day

Thursday, December 21st

With Emily at work and Amy in school, Adam found himself restless. He'd long since saturated himself with the books about Lucia, so he made his way to the public library and returned them. Sycamore Road, where it was located, made a semi-circle around the north part of town, so he decided to take a leisurely drive and take a fresh look at all the places and things that had become so familiar to him over the years.

The building that housed the local cleaners caught his eye a block away, so he made a quick right on South Central, and wheeled into the parking lot. Even though he'd been taking his suits there for over a decade, the architecture of the place left no mystery to the fact that it had once been a drive-in burger joint. He'd taken Emily there many a night on a date – they loved the privacy of being able to eat in the car, where they could talk about life and dreams and everything that lay ahead.

Looking around, he saw that the tan paint was beginning to peel away, showing the original red and white colors of the fast-food place. He thought about the fact that he and Emily had probably once been in the same parking space that he just pulled into, but years ago, long before their marriage, before Amy, before a lifetime of things that had happened. "Emily," he said aloud, "I'd give anything to go back and do them all over again."

He wasn't sure how long he sat there staring at the building, but he finally took a deep breath and put the car into reverse. The memories had been so strong that he sought out other landmarks of his youth: the Jackson Brothers Grocery on Mockingbird Lane where he'd sacked groceries as a boy; two blocks more and the Clinton Diner where he'd bussed tables for a year, named for the street, Clinton Way, instead of the Martin family that owned it; the city park on South Central Avenue where he and Emily had walked hand in hand so many times as newlyweds, taking bread crumbs to feed the ducks in the pond; and, of course, the cemetery. It took him a couple of minutes to get to the north side of town, where he turned onto Morning Glory Circle and drove through the front gates of Peaceful Hills Cemetery. As a young couple just dating, he and Emily had gone parking there, in the wooded area at the back that was away from the prying eyes of the public. It had other memories for him since, however; he navigated the narrow streets inside until he came to his parents' graves.

Adam left the car running, but walked over to them and knelt at the headstone. He took his fingers and traced their names that had been carved into the granite, then finally stood up and walked to the edge of the plot. A spotty snow covered the graves, adding a fitting visual to the cold feeling there. He turned back toward the stone, and said, "It's been so long, but I still miss you guys so very much." Adam choked for a minute, a tear welling up in his eye; finally, he was able to continue. "You know, I think that the most painful thing is when I really want to pick up the phone and call you about some little thing that happened during the day, and then realize that I can't...

that I'll never be able to again." He looked over at the two adjoining empty plots; ones that he and Emily had purchased a decade ago.

Taking a few steps, he stood on top of the place where his body would be laid to rest, sooner, obviously, rather than later. Looking back to his parents' graves, he said, "I... I guess that I'm going to be seeing you again pretty soon now. If there's any consolation to this whole thing that I've been going through, I guess that's one of the few perks."

He laughed at the absurdity of his monologue. Before leaving, though, he couldn't help but add one more thought. "You guys – if you can be there, when it happens, I mean – I'd love to have you greeting me on the other side. I don't know what to expect, even with everything Lucia's done to prepare me, but just knowing that when I die I'll see you again, well..." He was sobbing, and instead of trying to gather himself, he turned back toward the car and walked away, eyes on the ground.

He suddenly felt like he was being watched, and looked quickly up. Standing a few yards away from the car was a short man. He had a full head of hair, although it didn't appear to have been combed in a long time. The stubble of a beard covered most of his face, and he wore faded denim overalls and a blue work shirt. Smoke slowly curled up from a pipe that he clinched at the corner of his mouth.

"I'm sorry," Adam said, realizing the startled look that was probably on his face. "You kind of caught me off guard."

The man shrugged. "I'm Albert, the groundskeeper. Didn't mean to scare you. I always make my round this time of day to see if there's anything that needs attention. Not much does this time of year."

Adam's face flushed with embarrassment. "Yeah, well, you probably think that I'm crazy, standing out here crying, and talking to nobody."

111

"Buddy, if I thought that everyone that I saw carrying on a one-sided conversation here at the cemetery was crazy, I'd have to figure myself the only sane person in this town." He had pulled the pipe from his mouth, and was poking the stem toward Adam as he spoke, as if using it to emphasize every word. When he was finished, he started walking toward Adam. "I even saw the police chief out here one day, talking to one of the graves and cryin' like a baby. I've seen folks singing to their dearly departed, or yelling at them for leaving, and even having a picnic on the grave with a vacant place set. Naw, I've seen it all, and I can tell you that you ain't crazy." As he walked past Adam, he slapped him on the shoulder. "Besides, I don't believe that you were talking to nobody. I'm pretty sure that someone was listening. You take care, now."

Alone again, Adam stood there for a moment, nodded his head, and returned to the car.

As he pulled the driver's door closed, he heard the man's faint voice, "Yep, surprised what you see in a cemetery…"

* * * * *

A few blocks away, Adam drove past a lawn, and even though it was brown with winter and had patches of snow, it was dotted with well-manicured trees, and a sign that read *Colonial Pines*. For some reason that he couldn't explain, he slowed down. It was a nursing facility, or as his dad had called it, an old folks' home. He put on the brakes, and turned the car into the circle driveway. He couldn't help but feel compelled to stop… although he had no clue why.

Parking the car, he walked inside and was enveloped in the sterile scent of most hospitals and care institutions. The building had a round lobby, with hallways radiating out like a wagon wheel. A large, circular front desk was at the heart of the building, and nurses and workers there were moving around inside its confines with their daily tasks.

As Adam stood there silently for a moment, a thought suddenly crossed his mind. He walked to the front desk, approaching a woman in a set of pink scrubs typing at a keyboard as she watched a computer monitor. "Excuse me," he said.

It was a full minute before the woman looked up over the top of her glasses. "May I help you," she said, more of a statement than a question.

"Yes, I'm looking for Mr. Simmons; John Simmons, he was the principal at the high school years ago. I'm a former student, and I'm here for a visit."

"Corridor C," she said with a nod to her right. "Room five, on the right side."

Adam smiled. "Thanks for your help. I just thought that I'd–" He realized that she had stopped paying attention, and was once again typing and gazing down at the monitor. Looking around, he glanced at the large letters above each hallway, and walked off toward the third one.

Counting doors, he saw a number five above one on the right, and beside the door frame was a sign that read *Simmons, John.* Adam knocked on the door, and heard a male voice inside say, "Come in!" He turned the doorknob, and stepped inside.

The room was dim, with a fluorescent light mounted on the wall above a small institutional bed. There was a green recliner in the room positioned in front of a television on a stand, and a floor lamp just behind the chair. Narrow Venetian blinds shielded the light from the window on the far wall. A man stood looking out of the window, bending the blinds down with his hand just enough to peer outside.

Adam studied him; the man seemed somehow smaller than he remembered. What had it been, a decade or two? More

113

years perhaps – strange how living in the same city he had not crossed Simmons' path in all that time. Still, the figure before him seemed to be only a shadow of the man who once ruled the local high school with a firm hand, and struck fear into every student that walked the hallways during his tenure. His hair was thinning, non-existent on top, and tussled out on the sides as if it had never been combed. He was wearing a bathrobe over pajamas, and house slippers on his feet. Not knowing what to stay, Adam stood quietly for a moment.

"Well, young man, what have you done to warrant a trip to my office?" the old man's voice still boomed as Adam remembered. It jolted him for a moment, taking him back through the years. Simmons still gazed outside through the blinds on the window, but said, "Come on Adam, what is it this time? Talking in class, creating a disturbance? What infraction has brought you to my door?"

"Mr. Simmons, I…" Adam didn't know what to say. "This… this isn't your office, sir. This is…"

The old man turned and frowned. "Oh, hell, son, I'm just playing with you. I know this is a nursing home and I'm just one of its unwilling inmates. My horses haven't gone running that far around the bend – at least, not yet." He took a deep breath, and sighed. "So what brings young Adam to see his old principal?"

Adam laughed. "I'm not that young anymore, I'm afraid."

Mr. Simmons smiled, then took several laborious steps toward the recliner, and collapsed into it. "Perhaps… but I fear that I am indeed that old." He coughed violently into his hand, and then laid his head back against the chair. "Older and more worn out every day, it seems."

Forcing a smile, the younger man said, "You still look like that paddle-wielding giant to me, sir."

Shaking his head, Simmons said, "You know, boy, a fellow can be sent right to hell for lying to an old man."

114

Adam smiled again, genuinely this time. "I'm pretty sure that I'm not going to hell, sir."

The old man laughed out loud. "You know, I'd suspect that you're right about that." He chuckled again, and when his voice died out he paused, and then added, "But that doesn't answer my question – why are you here?"

Adam walked slowly over to the bed and sat down on the edge. He folded his hands, and rested his elbows on his knees. With a sigh, he said, "To be really honest, I don't have the slightest idea." After a few moments of awkward silence, he added, "I was out driving around, trying to sort a few things out, and just kind of turned into the parking lot. I don't know why. Then I remembered that I'd heard that you were, well…"

"You heard that my kids sold my house out from under me and threw me in this place?"

Adam opened his mouth, to speak, but nothing came out. He searched for a reply, but could not think of anything to say.

The man laughed, and then launched into another coughing fit. "Oh, don't worry," he finally said. "I don't blame them – not really. After all, look at me. As much as I hate to admit it, deep down inside I know that I can't be trusted to take care of myself. Certainly couldn't cook and clean up and all those things that used to be second nature. Besides, I suppose that the place isn't actually all that bad. As far as prisons go, that is."

Unconsciously Adam had been running his hand along the edge of the mattress; it was incredibly thin. The bed certainly wasn't comfortable to sit on – how in the world was Mr. Simmons sleeping on it every night?

"Yeah," the old man said, "I know, I know. If I could've picked out my own death-bed, it would have been a little different." He smiled. "I remember that old poet Robinson Jeffers, who wanted to die in his own room in his own bed." Simmons paused for a moment, smiled, and said, "Oh, that's right, mind you. I wasn't always a principal. I was one hell of an English Lit teacher for years. And Jeffers was my favorite poet… but where was I?" He looked away, then his head snapped back and he continued. "Right. Jeffers even built a long, narrow horizontal window beside his bed so that he could look out at the sea as he was dying. Later in life he wrote a poem about the bed by that window, and I wish I could remember it. All that comes to mind is the end – that it's going to sound like music to him when the patient one from the sea thumps his staff three times and calls, 'Come, Jeffers.'" Simmons sighed. "He gets that, I get this little hospital bed that no telling how many people have died in before me. Oh well, such is life." His eyes had drifted across the room, staring into a dim corner. He quickly looked back at Adam. "But you're not here for an old fellow's musings. Ask me what you're so desperate to know."

Shaking his head slowly from side to side, Adam said, "But Mr. Simmons, I don't know why I'm here. I certainly don't have a question in mind to–"

"Not even about death?"

The words took Adam by surprise, and almost stole his breath away. As he studied Simmons' face, he saw that the old man had an amused smile, and that his eyes were twinkling as if he knew a secret. After a moment, Adam managed to say, "A question about death? Wh–why would you ask that?"

Mr. Simmons leaned up in the chair, and pointed a bony finger toward Adam. "Surely you don't think that you're the first fellow to worry about death, do you son?" He laid his head against the back of the chair, and cackled. "Oh no, believe me, you're not. Life has a way of sneaking it up on you though… easing you into it when you're not looking." He clasped his hands, laid them in his lap, and stared away, lost for a moment. He finally continued. "I remember being a boy of seventeen when I first saw the specter of death before me. I'd stopped by the gas station where my best friend worked to drink a soda pop and visit a while; I would do that every day or so. Anyway, he started tell me about how his granddaddy had died and he was going to Dallas for the funeral. For some reason, it struck me hard – like someone had hit me with a hammer between the eyes – that I was going to die someday. Even though I was a kid, I couldn't shake the fear that was running through my mind. I was days getting over that feeling – the knowledge that I was going to die, and there was nothing at all that I could do about it. I felt helpless." He closed his eyes for a moment. "But I was a child; I knew that I had a whole lifetime before I had to worry about it, so I pushed it to the back of my mind. Know what happened next?" he asked.

Adam shook his head, and softly said, "No."

The grin that crossed Mr. Simmons' face was somehow sad. "Well, you blink your eyes, and you're graduating high school. Blink them again, and you're out of college. Again and you're married and planning a family. That's what happened to my wife Maggie and me. We were going to build a bigger house, but we thought that we'd hold off until the kids grew up a bit. We were going to go on vacation, but decided to wait until we could save up more money. Years went by, our children became adults, and our hair began to turn gray. We had always talked about going to the State Fair that we'd heard so much about, but every year it just wasn't convenient. As much as we wanted to go, we'd always put it off another year. Then Maggie went to the doctor with a pain in her gut that just wouldn't go away, and three months later I was burying her over at the cemetery. A few more years went by, the school board thought that I was getting a little old, and they wanted to bring a young man in with new ideas. They gave me a reception and a wooden plaque with an engraved metal plate that had my name and said *World's Greatest Educator* underneath, and then booted me out of the front door."

Glancing around the room, Adam asked, "So do you still have the plaque?"

Laughing, Simmons said, "Nope. You see, I laid it out in my back yard in the grass just off the patio, and for the next couple of years I'd go out every night before bed and piss on it. I finally figured even that was giving it too much attention, so I picked it up one day, drove to the grocery store, and threw it into the dumpster out back. Who knows; maybe someone will excavate it out of the landfill a thousand years from now and figure that I really was the world's greatest educator... maybe they'll build a statue in my honor."

Adam laughed with him, shook his head, "Stranger things have happened." They finally sat in silence for a few moments, until he said, "But all that Mr. Simmons, you didn't tell me why you thought I was seeking answers about death."

"Aren't we all?" he replied softly.

"I wasn't." Adam shifted on the bed, and chose his words carefully before continuing. "At least, not until a few days ago."

The old man went into another coughing fit, and after calming, finally wiped his mouth and said, "So what happened – did someone tell you that death was stalking you?"

Adam studied him. "Why do I get the feeling that we're doing some kind of weird little dance here, Mr. Simmons?" He paused, and then added, "Let me ask you outright. Do you know about Lucia?"

Mr. Simmons leaned forward, his eyes dancing with life in contrast to his frail body. "Lucia? No, I don't know the name. But I can tell you something?" He reached out and grabbed Adam's hand, leaning out so far that it seemed that he might topple out of the chair. "Adam, the world is magic. Really, really magic. All sorts of wonderful, incredible things exist in the world around us, but we spend most of our lives unable – or unwilling – to see them." He grasped Adam's hand tighter. "Sometimes I think that it's one of God's little jokes – as children, our eyes are open to the wonder of the world that He created for us. As we grow and mature, however, we think ourselves so learned and wise that we dismiss all those wondrous things as a child's fantasy. We seek to define the world, and even God himself, with our own thoughts and words. The thing is, Adam, as we get to the 'September of our years' as Ol' Blue Eyes so eloquently put it all those years ago, you change. You start to remember, and accept, the magic of the world that you held as a child."

Adam smiled. "A blessing of old age?"

"And a curse. You realize how much of your life that you wasted being 'learned and wise'. How much you could have done if you were only able to look beyond the walls of reality that you spend your life erecting around yourself." The old man sighed. "What a waste." After a moment he added, "Ah, to do it all again. How different I would be."

With a laugh, Adam said, "You mean the hard-assed principal might have been a softy?"

"No…" he said, unwavering, "I wouldn't change my way of thinking as an instructor – young ones like you needed a firm hand guiding them." Pausing, Simmons said, "But in my personal life, well, I don't think that I'd be so staunch and rigid. Perhaps I wouldn't have missed as much."

"Okay," Adam asked, "so I'm a little lost here. What is it that you missed?"

Mr. Simmons just stared at him for a moment, then leaned forward, put out his hand, and rested it on Adam's knee. "My friend, I missed out on the magic of life." He patted Adam's knee a few times, then sat back.

"So you're saying that I should embrace this 'magic' of life?" Adam asked.

The old man nodded slowly. "That's exactly what I'm saying."

"So how do I do that?"

Simmons smiled. "Maybe that's something that you should ask your 'Lucia'."

Adam was still for a minute, and said, "But I thought you didn't know anything about her.

"I don't – but from what you said earlier… and the way that you said it… she seems to be someone that's very important to you," he said somberly. "Besides," he added, "I'm an old man. What do I have to offer someone like yourself?"

Adam glanced down at his watch, stood up, and put his hand on the man's shoulder. "Quite a lot, I'm certain. And I don't think that you're telling me everything that you know." He turned and walked back toward the door. Pausing, he looked back and said, "If you don't mind, maybe I'll drop back in from time to time – just to check on you. For as long as I can, anyway."

"I'll be here," Mr. Simmons said with a sad smile. "And Adam?"

"Yes," he said pausing.

"You know that I was once the age that you are now."

Adam shrugged. "Of course."

"Know how long ago that was?"

Instead of trying to do the math, Adam simply said, "How long?"

Simmons raised his hand, and snapped his fingers. "That long ago."

Pausing, and then nodding slowly, Adam walked into the hallway, and shut the door.

* * * * *

120

The evening was cold, and the snow was starting to fall again – a light dusting in miniscule flakes. At midnight, Adam was standing underneath the eve of the house with Elvis tucked safely at his feet.

Minutes passed – he didn't know how many – and he finally said, "Lucia?"

The darkness was instantly illuminated as she appeared on the patio. Elvis lost no time in running over to greet her. She patted his head and rubbed his ears, and then said, "Adam, you don't have to huddle underneath the eve of your house – come out here and talk to me."

He took a tentative step out, and found that in the aura of her light the snow was not falling. "How do you do that?"

"It has just been made comfortable for you," she said. Bending down to pet the basset hound once again, she added, "And for this little one."

"So you control the weather?"

"I control nothing. God controls everything."

"Okay, whatever. I've stopped being amazed at all the things that have been happening."

A smile crossed Lucia's young face, and she said, "So, did you have a pleasant day?"

"Well, an odd one." Adam said. "But I suppose that you know that already."

Her smile remained, but the young lady said nothing.

With a deep sigh, Adam began. "Okay, I'm not sure how to start. I went out to the cemetery today and talked to my parents…"

"How very strange – why would you go there?"

He raised his palms. "Hey, I know that they're not really there. I guess that seeing their headstone is just a solid reminder of them. Sounds crazy, I know, but if I can't see them, I can see their grave, and well, I guess that's something for me to lock onto."

121

"But you can talk to them anywhere," Lucia said.

Adam's head snapped around toward her. "You mean... you mean that my parents can hear me?"

She smiled again. "I did not say that. God hears you anywhere, anytime, and beyond that, things that happen are only in accordance to his will."

"So then they can't hear me," he said, disappointed.

"But I did not say that, either. I just know that if it was not at God's bidding, I would not know about you, your family, Elvis the precious dog, pickup trucks, or anything else that we have conversed about over the last few nights."

He rubbed his eyes with his hand. "I'm so very confused, Lucia."

"Of course you are," she said pleasantly, as if referring to the weather instead of heavenly matters. "But remember, you don't have the capacity to understand God and His ways."

"Okay, fine. But I've got my question ready, and while it's not quite about death, I could make the argument that it really is. I also really, really want to know the answer."

"I am curious," Lucia said. "What is your question, then?"

"Well, today I went to visit..."

"Mr. Simmons," Lucia said, completing his sentence.

"Man! I hate it when you do that." Adam rubbed his hands over his face. "Do you know everything that I'm about to say?"

A slight smile crossed her face. "Only what God tells me. Nothing more."

"Okay, so you may know that Mr. Simmons turned out to be a much more spiritual man than I could have ever imagined." After a moment, Adam added, "He said that the world was magic... is that right?"

Lucia stood there for a minute, and said, "Perhaps a bit of a stretch for your question, but I will answer. Is the world – as Mr. Simmons said – magic?" She smiled. "Yes. A very easy answer this evening." With that, the young woman turned and began to walk away.

"Whoa, Lucia, hey!" Adam quickly said. "Don't leave!"

She looked puzzled. "But why? You asked a question, and I have answered it."

"But Lucia, I have so many more questions – you can't just ignore me!"

Turning back, she said, "Very well. What else would you like to know?"

"Look," he started, "I've led a very normal, natural life up to this point. All of a sudden you come into my life, I find out that I'm dying, and the world is looking more and more... well... strange to me." He took a minute and walked around the back yard. "You just confirmed that the world is a supernatural place – what am I supposed to think?"

She stared at him for a moment. "Adam, most people realize how special the earthly world is only as they depart it in death. You've been given a special gift, and more, by learning that it is much more. Isn't that enough?"

"No!" he replied passionately. "No, it's not! I want to know more!"

Lucia smiled. "Then trust in God, look to Him, but most importantly, talk to Him. Just like I told you a few nights ago. But you asked me if the world was magic... it is, and appreciating that 'magic', as you put it, comes from understanding how active God is in your life. A few nights ago we talked about the supernatural, and believe me, the world is a supernatural place. It is far, far beyond the 'natural' that most people imagine. Since humans are incapable of understanding it, they categorize everything that they cannot comprehend as evil or sinful. It is not, though – God's creation contains much more than the human eye can see or the human hand touch. Angels are everywhere, and so is God, and the power that He has for all humans is there for them to tap into. But they have to be able to have faith to do that... to really command that mountain to move. Can you do that?"

Adam hesitated, and said, "I don't know." He looked into Lucia's eyes. "But in the short time that I have left, is that really important?"

Without hesitating, she said, "Perhaps now, more than ever." She then turned and walked away.

Adam sighed, unsure of what to think of their conversation.

The Tenth Day

Funeral homes always gave Adam the creeps. He glanced down the hallway where the staterooms were, and a chill went through his body. He shook his head, and wondered which one his body would be displayed in.

For a moment he could envision Emily and standing out in the lobby with some of the family members, receiving guests during the visitation as they came to pay their respects.

He took a deep breath, shook off the vision, and walked toward the office. A young man sat at a desk, typing information on a computer. "May I help you, sir?" he said with a smile. All morticians seemed to muster that same expression on demand – friendly, yet somber, with a touch of comfort and caring. Maybe it was part of their training.

"Hi, I was hoping to catch Mr. Morgan for a quick minute. Is he in?"

A large man entered through a doorway that led into the other offices. "Perfect timing – I was just coming back from lunch." He extended his hand.

As Adam shook it, the man gave him the same smile that the young man had. "And what can I do for you today... Adam, I believe it is? Yes, Adam, I helped you and your wife with funeral pre-need planning a few years ago."

He nodded. "That's right – my wife's mother had just died without having any plans made, and it was an extra burden on Emily at a time when she was already overcome with grief."

"As I recall, it was a beautiful service, though." He motioned toward the door. "Come into my office so that we can talk." The big man turned and led Adam down a short hallway and into an office with a dark mahogany desk, off-white walls, and landscape paintings of peaceful scenes tastefully hung. The only sign of the daily grief experienced there was the box of tissues that rested on the desk, and every table in the room.

"You know, Adam, it was wise of you folks to do the pre-need planning. Most people put it off, as if that will somehow keep death away from them." He paused, looking somberly at Adam. "But death can come at any time."

"Someone else has been telling me much the same thing," Adam said. "And that's why I'm here. I just wanted to check and make sure that everything is in order with our... our accounts, I guess. You know, that everything has been picked out, chosen, paid for, all that. If something were to happen to me I'd want it to be as easy on Emily as possible."

"Of course." Mr. Morgan looked to the computer screen on the side of his desk, and began typing. A mouse click or so later, he nodded his head. "Everything is in order. Your plans were paid off a few years ago, the caskets and vaults have been selected, you've selected the plots at the cemetery, and I'm showing that even the headstone has been chosen. Other than planning the services themselves, you're as prepared as you can be."

"So I'm ready to go," Adam said.

Morgan only allowed himself a thin smile at the jest. "Well, so to speak."

Adam sat silently for a moment, and then said, "What about the service – can I go ahead and plan that out?"

"Hmmm… I seem to remember a rather unique suggestion that you had when you and your wife were here before. Not one that I'll soon forget – that's why I recognized you when you came in."

After a chuckle, Adam said, "Yeah, that's right, but I was just playing around with Emily. She was so freaked out by doing all that in the first place that I was just trying to lighten the mood."

The large man leaned back in the leather chair, and it seemed to whisper a groan in protest. "Let's see if I can recall it exactly… a 'Viking funeral' if I'm not mistaken."

Adam shrugged. "That was it."

"We were to take a wooden rowboat out to the lake, fill it with gasoline-soaked kindling wood, then place your body on top and launch the boat. When it got far enough from shore, one of your bow-hunting friends – his name escapes me – would shoot a flaming arrow out to ignite the boat and its cargo, and everyone would drink beer and sing your favorite songs until the boat and your cremated body slipped below the surface."

"Yep, that's about how I remember it," he said with a sheepish grin.

"As I pointed out at the time, that would be highly illegal, not only in this state but in every one in which I am versed in the interment laws."

"I remember you saying that, too."

Mr. Morgan shook his head and smiled. "Well, barring any funeral plans of that nature, anything that you could note would probably be helpful to your wife should you precede her in death. Just notes, mind you. The plans might not be relevant at the time that they are needed, but they could serve as a guideline."

Adam looked confused. "What do you mean, 'not relevant' – that Emily might not want to do them?"

He raised his hand slightly, as if to comfort Adam. "Of course not; but you appear to be a healthy man, and decisions that you make now may not be applicable when the time comes. For example, the person that you choose to officiate at the funeral might be a pastor who's long since moved on to a different church. Or decades from now, some of the pallbearers that you've chosen might have already passed. That kind of thing."

"Oh... okay, I see what you're saying." Adam sat back in the chair, staring at a painting of a serene mountain for a few moments. He didn't want to correct the funeral director, but in his current situation, all plans would be relevant. He imagined Emily sitting in that very chair across the desk from Mr. Morgan in the near future... days, maybe a week or so? Who knew. Adam smiled sadly; Morgan would probably give her that comforting smile, and say, "You know, it is very odd – Adam came in not long ago just to check on the status of all the pre-need planning. What a strange coincidence."

* * * * *

"Adam, I've been your insurance agent for, what, fifteen years now? Trust me, everything is in order. I've got you covered in every possibility from a car wreck to a tornado taking your house to Oz. You're fine."

Nodding, Adam said, "Okay, that sounds good, but what if something happens to me – what if I was to die?"

Jerry Burkman picked up the manila folder from the desk held it up, and said, "When you called and said that you wanted to stop by I reviewed all your information. You and your wife both have a supplemental policy that will kick in if something happens to either one of you, and I know that your job has a very generous insurance package – even if it's not through me."

He squirmed in his chair. "Okay, so let's assume something happened to me. What all would Emily have to do?"

Burkman sighed. "Well, not much. If anything did happen – God forbid – I'd hear about it and get in touch with her. You know that I'd try to take as much of the burden off her as possible. She'd just need to sign a couple of things, provide a death certificate for the home office, and I'd push the rest of the paperwork through. She'd have a check in, oh, six weeks at the outside."

"Okay. That will work." Adam took a deep breath, and then looked back to his insurance agent. "Look, Jerry, you've got to promise me something. I've got to have your word on this."

Burkman folded his hands in front of him on the desk, and his brow furrowed. "Okay… on what?"

"If something happens to me, go see Emily as soon as you can. She'll be upset, but I want her to know that she has someone who's going to be helping her with all of the financial stuff. Tell her that the key to the safe-deposit box at the bank is on my key ring. As soon as she's able, she needs to go get the papers out of it and bring them home. She'll find our insurance policies, our certificates of deposit, a copy of our wills, and a letter that I put in there earlier today with some funeral information. Tell her to read the letter from me, bring the insurance information to you, and then take everything else back and put it in the box after she's looked through it all."

"Of course I will, Adam… but you're kind of creeping me out here. You're not that much older than me, and I certainly plan on living a lot longer. You should, too. What gives?"

Snapping his fingers, Adam added, "Oh, and I almost forgot. Tell her to call our Human Resources Director at my work to get all of my company insurance things rolling. She's met Janice and should remember her, but remind Emily to make the call as soon as possible."

Burkman stood up and walked around the desk, taking a seat on the corner and crossing his arms. "Adam, you can be assured that in such a case I'll do everything possible to help Emily; so will my wife. We'll be right there to take care of anything that we can. But you haven't answered my question – what the hell is going on?"

Adam stood up. "You heard that Ben Robertson died, right?"

"Of course; like I said, it's a small town. I've already been working with Mary on his affairs."

Sighing, Adam said, "Well, it was just so sudden and unexpected. Ben and I are the same age, and it got me to thinking that maybe I'd better get all my ducks in a row... just in case, you know? Once I did, I wouldn't have to worry about it." He put out his hand for Jerry to shake. "Trust me, nothing is wrong," he lied.

With a handshake, Burkman said, "Well, it's something that we all should do; you never know. But I'm sure that you're going to out-live me and half the town."

"Your lips to God's ears," Adam said, and turned to leave.

* * * * *

"I understand that you've had a busy day," Lucia said.

The voice and brilliance of her light came suddenly and simultaneously, startling Adam. After a moment's recovery, he said, "I suppose that I have. It's been a good day, though... I mean, as well as it can be when you're preparing to die."

130

Lucia showed no emotion, and said, "These are good preparations for any person to make, no matter what the situation is."

"I guess. I probably should have been on checking on my affairs every few years anyway. But it's done."

She stood there silently, waiting.

With everything that I've been doing, there's one thing that I can't get off my mind. I have a question related to all this that I want to ask you tonight."

"I am ready," she said, gently folding her hands and looking into Adam's eyes.

"Okay, here goes. After I'm gone, will Emily and Amy be all right?" After a moment, a single tear rolled down his cheek. "With the things that I've done today, all for them, I can't help but think about it. I've got people to help with the funeral arrangements, and with all the insurance stuff, but I need to know about them as my family. I have to know if they're going to be able to make it without me."

Looking confused, she answered, "How could I know that? I cannot see into the future, other than what God tells me. I know that they are both strong, but their reaction to the inevitable is something that I cannot predict."

Shaking his head, Adam said, "But you've got to know – or you've got to ask. It's something that I can't get off my mind. How can I face death without knowing whether or not they can go on?"

Lucia took a deep breath, looked away, and then finally back at him. "Adam, suppose that I brought Emily this news and not you. If she died, would you survive?"

"I can't imagine losing my wife. If she were to die, it would completely devastate me. I wouldn't want to go on..." he stopped for a moment, and then added, "...but I'd have to be strong for Amy. She and I would keep going, as painful as it might be."

Smiling, Lucia said, "Then I am confident that the same would be true for Emily. The two of you have been together for all these years, solving problems, fighting whatever adversity came your way, conquering life's problems, and bringing up a wonderful daughter in the process. Your strength is her strength, and hers yours. I would imagine that she would be fine, and that you can ally any fears about such matters."

He nodded slowly. "You know, I believe that you're right. But if you can't definitively answer that question, how about this: is there any way that I can come back to visit her after I have died? You know, just to make sure that she's okay?"

The girl raised her eyebrows, considered the question. She finally said, "That is a difficult question. Clearly the chasm between the living and those who have passed can be traversed." She shrugged her shoulders and smiled. "Just look at me."

As she spoke, Elvis pushed his way through the curtains and walked onto the patio. "Always a welcome party to our discussions," Lucia said. She bent down and beckoned the dog to come to her, which he did, and was rewarded with a scratch behind his ear. Straightening up, she said, "Let me say this; all things happen at God's will. Nothing can occur otherwise. Yet man tries to understand God by making up rules to describe His ways. I am afraid that your motion picture industry does nothing to help this, with their stories of souls stuck on Earth because they cannot 'find the light'. Nonsense. Can you imagine God allowing a soul to be blocked from its destination?" She shook her head. "Haunted houses, ghost-hunting in cemeteries, all lunacy. The fact is that in some circumstances God allows souls to return for various reasons, just as He gives his angels passage between the worlds to accomplish their tasks."

Adam looked at her, smiling. "Remember that I first thought that you were an angel."

132

"That is correct, you did. But as I said last night, the world is magic – I was apprehensive about that description at first, but I have come to think that is one of the best ways that I know to describe it. Angels are around you every day; you see them all the time without recognizing them. The spirits of those that have died can return as well, as God allows. All are at the behest of God, and are operating within His will." She paused, and added, "Even God himself comes down to walk among his children."

"God? Really?" Adam seemed to be thrown by the revelation. "Why would He do that?"

"Because He loves His creation – He loves His children. And in a human form, they can interact with Him."

"Wow. Do you..." Adam said thoughtfully, "do you think that I've ever seen Him?"

Lucia smiled. "To be honest, most people have. They just do not realize it. He doesn't appear as an old, distinguished man in a long white beard, wearing a brilliant, shining robe. He might be a homeless-looking person outside of the grocery, or a bank teller that you've never seen before."

"Wow. That's hard to imagine." He was shaking his head, as if to allow the thought to get through. "But can I come back? I mean, if Emily needs me?"

She shut her eyes momentarily, and then opened them to look directly at Adam. "That is not for me to decide, but even if you did, would your wife be open to it? The world is filled with so many wonderful, magical things placed there by God, yet humans are so closed-minded that they refuse to even contemplate them. Your experience with me has probably opened yours, but what would open your wife's mind to the possibility?"

"I don't know," Adam said, his tone a bit sad. "I wish that I could make her understand all this."

"God gives all this to His children. Not all are willing to accept it. Most people try to create God in their own image, making Him fit into their beliefs. They attempt to lock God in a box of their own design. A foolish – and sad – endeavor." She turned and began to walk away, and then stopped. "But it may be that while you will not come back to your wife, God might call on you to visit another human to give him a gift, and answer a number of questions…"

"Now you're joking with me, Lucia."

She looked back and said, "Perhaps not. Goodnight Adam." Looking down at the basset hound, she added, "And goodnight, my precious." Suddenly, Lucia was gone.

The Eleventh Day

When Adam was a kid, the front door to the church was always unlocked. In those days it never occurred to him that it would be otherwise. Still, the world had changed so much, and Adam was shocked to turn the doorknob and easily push the front door open.

The church was warm inside, and looked exactly as it had the last time that he was there – for Mr. Franklin's funeral ten years ago. Adam started up the aisle, but then stopped by the back row of pews where he'd spent so many Sunday mornings sitting next to his parents.

A head poked out of a door at the front of the church by the piano. "Adam? Why, is that you?"

The man's short-cropped white hair was a tip-off that it was Reverend James. The pastor had worn his hair in a snowy crew-cut since Adam been a child. He mused that even back then, Rev. James had seemed old. "Good morning, Pastor. Am I catching you in the middle of something?" Adam said, raising his hand in greeting.

135

"No, no, just going over my sermon for tomorrow morning. Come on back," he said, disappearing back through the door. "It's certainly good to see you in church!"

Adam walked up the main aisle, turned to the left, and took the door that led into a hallway. Directly across the hall was the entrance to the pastor's office, a small room with overflowing bookshelves lining the walls. Rev. James sat at his desk, leaning back in the chair, smiling. "I think that the only places that I've seen you for years now are at the store, post office, or bank."

Pulling out the visitor's chair in front of the desk, Adam sat down. "Yeah, I guess that it's been a while."

Both men were silent, and it became more awkward with each passing moment. Finally, the Reverend said, "So, to what do I owe the pleasure?"

Adam gave a heavy sigh. "Well, you've been my pastor here all my life, even though I don't attend very regularly any more. You baptized me and performed my wedding to Emily."

The white-haired man nodded. "All true. And it was all my genuine pleasure."

"Okay, so, I have a question for you." Adam struggled for the words, and finally just said what was on his mind: "Rev. James, if I were to die, would I go to heaven?"

The pastor's eyes narrowed, studying the younger man across the desk from him. "Adam, I'd approach my answer this way. I preached the sermon on the Sunday night when you gave your life to the Lord. I counseled with you, took you through several weeks of baptism school, and then actually performed the immersion myself. I watched you grow in the church, give your tithes, and even though you've been backsliding for a number of years, I'd say that there is no question that you would enter the gates of heaven when you die." He paused, and his brow crinkled. "Why in the world would you ask something like that?"

Adam gave his shoulders an exaggerated shrug. "Oh, as every year goes by I get a little older, and I guess that the question presses on me a little more as I get closer to my death. And, well, I really haven't been coming to church in a while…"

Rev. James leaned forward and folded his hands on the desk. "It all comes down to doctrine, Adam. In our church, we don't feel that humans can fall from grace – in other words, once you've been saved, you can't become un-saved. It's like a bell; you can't un-ring it once it's been rung. There are some churches that preach the idea that if you're not faithful and true to their church, you can fall from salvation." He chuckled a little, and added, "You know, there are even some folks like the church just up the road, that believe everyone who's not a member of their church is going to spend eternity in hell. The thing that amuses me is that every month or so, the pastor of that church and I have lunch over at the diner. I can't help but be amazed at the fact that he sits down to eat with me, while fully believing that my congregation and I will all burn in hell for time everlasting."

Adam leaned forward, resting his arms on his knees. "So do you think that they'll be the ones going to hell?"

The Reverend sat for a moment, smiled and said, "You know, that's something that our faith more or less ignores. We don't pass judgment on any other denomination; we just focus on our own."

"But what makes us right and them wrong?"

Leaning back in his chair, the pastor said, "Adam, I'm going to tell you something. Now this is going to be just between me and you. The moment that you leave this office, I'll give my word that this conversation never took place – that I never said these things."

Adam's eyes narrowed as he studied the pastor, wondering what he was about to say.

"Now I know that a preacher's not supposed to lie," he continued. "But if ever asked about this," a grin crossed the man's face, "I'm gonna lie like a lazy dog. Understand?"

Nodding his head, Adam said, "I think so."

"Good. So there's no use to go around telling people that I said all this." He leaned forward again, folding his hands together on the desk. "That other pastor that I told you about having lunch with? Well, it's not just him that I differ with in theology. You see, we have a ministerial alliance here in town that's made up of all of the pastors of all the churches – it's not a big town, you know, so there's only fourteen of us. We meet once a month, discuss community happenings, plan church participation in events like the Fourth of July, that kind of thing. We never, ever discuss religion... and for a good reason." He paused for a minute, studying Adam. "You see, if I go around the table in my mind, I can see all sorts of conflicts. This pastor believes everyone else is going to hell because you have to take communion with their group to be saved. The next fellow thinks that you have to be baptized – in their church, mind you – to be saved; in fact, if you did without that baptism, even if you've become a Christian, it's straight to hell for you. Another pastor believes that still another one is violating scripture because his denomination sprinkles for baptism instead of immersing. We even have a woman pastor in the group, and pretty much everyone believes that she and her flock are going to hell because many teach that women are supposed to be silent in the church." He shrugged his shoulders. "Truth is, all this is dogma is made up by man – Jesus never taught any of it. I believe that salvation is by God's grace alone, and nothing else that you do, whether it's getting baptized, taking the Lord's Supper, never missing a Sunday, handling snakes, you name it, none of it can make a difference in salvation."

After a moment, Adam asked, "So why all the different beliefs?"

The pastor smiled, although he looked a little sad. "Well, Adam, here's the problem. It takes faith to rely completely on God for salvation by grace, and I hate to say it, but faith is not in man's nature. It's almost impossible for him to give up all control, even to God. Because of that, at least to my way of thinking, over the years we've invented these little things that we control that allow us to find salvation, and different denominations have embraced different ones. Never miss a Sunday, and you go to heaven. Take the Lord's Supper every week, and you go to heaven. Get baptized, and you go to heaven. All these, and the countless others that we've come up with, are things that we as man can do to supposedly control our own salvation. It's not Biblical, though, and Jesus never talked about any of them. Yet we embrace them as absolute doctrine because as men, it gives us some control..." He sighed, and added, "And takes some of the control away from God; at least in our own eyes."

After a moment of silent contemplation, Adam said, "But that sound ridiculous. How could things have gotten so out of hand?"

The pastor shook his head. "Easy – because religion is run by man. Man makes the rules, interprets the Bible, and decides what God wants and doesn't want, likes and doesn't like. Basically, we try to create God in our own image. And because of that, you have all these different religious groups who believe that they've got the market on truth cornered, and that everyone else is wrong."

"Okay," Adam said, "so what do you believe?"

"Again, this is a conversation that we never had – don't forget that. But what I believe is that no one belief is absolutely correct, no matter what any one of them might think. Not even mine. But God Himself knows that we're imperfect beings, so

He allows us to muddle along in our various ways. I think that everyone sitting around the table at the ministerial alliance is equally capable of going to heaven. And when you asked me earlier about yourself, well," he stopped, took a deep breath, and appeared a bit reflective for a moment. "Adam, you're a good man, your faith and belief in the Lord seems sincere, and even though you aren't attending church very regularly, I wouldn't worry about your eternal destination... for whatever my opinion is worth."

"But shouldn't you know?"

Shaking his head, the pastor said, "Only God himself is the judge. He knows everyone's hearts, their minds, their souls. So keep focused on Him, and you'll be fine. Although it wouldn't hurt for you to come back to church occasionally."

He sat up, and then stood. "I'll keep that in mind, Rev. James, seriously, I will. Thanks for giving me a few moments of your time."

The pastor stood and extended his hand. "Anytime, son, anytime at all. You know, I'd be very happy to pray with you before you go."

Adam shook his hand, and said, "Naw, I'm good. I do think that I'd like to sit out in the sanctuary for a few minutes, if that's okay."

"You're always welcome in God's house, Adam. I'll be here going over my sermon if you need anything at all."

"Thanks," Adam said with a nod, and then headed out of the office. He suddenly stopped, and stepped back inside. "One thing – what you just told me made a lot of sense. Wouldn't an attitude like that promote harmony among different churches? I mean, why not preach that from the pulpit?"

"If I did that, Adam, I wouldn't have a pulpit to preach from." He rocked back in his chair, and folded his hands behind his head. "I feel a genuine calling to shepherd this group of people as best as I can. Do I completely agree with all

140

of the tenants of our denomination? No – I have questions, like many people do. But at the end of the day, if I'm able to help my people in their spiritual lives, then I'm comfortable that I'm doing my job."

After a moment, Adam nodded, and then turned to leave.

As he did, Rev. James added, "Don't forget – this conversation never took place."

Adam didn't answer, but instead smiled and went back into the sanctuary, walked back down the aisle, and took a seat on the back pew. He rested his head on the back of the pew in front of him, and began to silently speak to God.

* * * * *

It was a few minutes before midnight, and Adam had gone outside for his nightly conference. They'd turned in early, though, and Emily was fast asleep. He couldn't wait to talk to Lucia.

As he slowly, quietly slid the glass door closed, a basset's nose poked out. "Oh, how silly of me. I wouldn't want to do this without you." Opening the door a little, Elvis came bounding outside, looked around, and then plopped down on the patio.

Adam walked out into the yard, his footsteps crunching in the snow, and stopped at the back fence. It was a beautiful night, and the moonlight seemed to illuminate everything with a soft glow.

"Good evening, Adam."

He turned, and from the other side of the fence Lucia's brilliance was just starting to fade down to a manageable level.

"It's a good evening, I guess. I mean, it's been kind of a confusing day." He glanced out into the distance for a few moments, gathering his thoughts. "I went to see the pastor of the church I go to." After a minute, he added, "Well, I mean, that I sometimes go to."

"I know," she said softly.

Adam's brow furrowed. "You know? Are all of my daily activities the topic of conversation in Heaven?"

She smiled and shook her head. "No. Just between God and me. He tells me what I need to know for our nightly discussions."

He put his hands up to cover his face, heaved a deep sigh through his fingers, and finally let them drop. "Lucia, you're wearing me out with this 'talking to God' thing. It's like He's just some guy hanging out at the local drug store that you converse with over a cup of coffee."

The girl looked upward, as if contemplating an answer. Finally, she said, "Your comparison is not that far from the truth. Although, He is certainly not a man – He is God. But He created man in His image, so why wouldn't we be able to converse with Him." After a moment, she added, "You spoke to Him today, in fact."

"True, I did stop for a bit of prayer, but it was hardly a conversation."

Elvis made a slow circle around her, and Lucia smiled again. "You spoke, and God listened... and then thought about what you had to say."

Adam glanced quickly to her. "You've said that kind of thing before, but what do you mean? Why would He think about what I said?"

"As I also told you before, because God not only hears your prayers, He acts on them. Not always in the way that you might want Him to, of course."

"I guess I still don't understand," Adam said, shaking his head.

Lucia looked down as though deep in thought, took a few paces, and then turned to face Adam. "Your beautiful daughter

Amy… suppose that she asked for you for an automobile as a Christmas present. Would you buy it for her?"

Caught off guard, Adam guffawed. "I should say not – for any number of reasons!"

"Of course," Lucia said with a melancholy smile. "But suppose that she was a young woman going off to college and needed a reliable form of transportation, would you do it then?"

"In a heartbeat," he answered flatly. "But you knew that already, didn't you?"

Her smile widened. "I did, I must admit. So while you would deny her this object at one time because it would be irresponsible and even dangerous, at another time you would present it to her without hesitation."

Adam nodded. "I'm not dumb, Lucia. I can see where you're headed with this."

"Good. Because the things that you ask God for sometimes would be worse for you in a particular instance, whether it looks like it or not. And of course, there are other times when your desires simply don't fit into God's plan, as much as He hates to disappoint His children."

"Okay, but shouldn't His plan benefit His children?"

Lucia paused again. "Such a simple concept, but one that is so difficult for arrogant man to understand," she finally said, taking a few steps out into the snowy yard.

Adam opened his palms, surprised. "So you're calling me arrogant now? I didn't think that you were in the name-calling and judging business."

She laughed aloud. "Oh Adam, you are so frustrating to me sometimes, and it's a feeling that I no longer tend to have!" Walking back to him, Lucia said, "It is not you – it is mankind. All women and men! You reach a point of supposed maturity, of knowledge, of security. You talk to God as His peer, when in fact the relationship that you have with your young child is a

143

much more perfect example of God's relationship with you. As wise as people think that they are, when compared to the Almighty, they are but children. You question God's ways in the same way a child questions his or her parent. The family might have to move to another city for a parent to take a new job, forcing the child to leave friends and familiar circumstances. Even though it would be better for the entire family in the end, the child cannot begin to see it. Or perhaps a young girl is made to wear braces to correct a dental problem – it is a catastrophe in her eyes, unaware of the benefits that will come. But the young aren't able to begin to comprehend the world that they live in like their parents are. In that same way, you can never comprehend God's ways."

A spark surged through Adam. "Even when He's going to kill a father who loves his family, and throw their lives into disarray – into complete and total hell?" His voice rose with every word.

"Adam…" Lucia shook her head, took a deep breath, and stared into the night. Finally she turned back. "First of all, as loved as you are, you have no idea what might happen to your family without you. You forget that God loves them as much as He loves you. Even if you are gone, He will keep His eyes on them. But even more than that, you minimize what your life will be after your death. Would you dare to compare your day to day existence with mine? You have no idea the wonder that awaits you." Again she shook her head, and began to walk away.

"Wait!" Adam called after her. "I didn't get to ask my question tonight."

She looked back and somberly said, "I believe that you have asked several questions in our exchange this evening."

He held up his index finger, pointing upward, and said, "But not an official question."

144

Turning around, she stared at him for a moment, and finally said, "Very well. Ask your question."

Adam took a deep breath. "Okay, here goes. We were talking about my church a moment ago. While I was there, I asked my pastor whether or not I'd go to heaven, and he told me that I would."

"A foolish answer on his part," she said, her face peaceful. "Only God can judge – not man."

"Yeah, he said that too. But that's not my question, although it does kind of stem from it – my pastor couldn't tell me, but I want to know which religion, denomination, faith, whatever you want to call it, is the correct one. If I'm dying, I want to be able to embrace the correct one."

A puzzled look crossed Lucia's face. "If you are contemplating your own death, why waste a question on such a philosophical topic? It has been debated by scholarly humans throughout the centuries... why pose that question to me, now, at this time?"

"Because," Adam began, "my amnesty is more or less over tomorrow night. Lucia, I don't know if I'll have another day, another week, another month... but with whatever time I have, I want to find the church that God favors. I want to worship Him there, and not waste whatever time I might have left worshiping in other ways. Do I need to take communion? Or get baptized a different way? I heard what my pastor had to say, and he sounded pretty convincing, but you talk to God – he doesn't. At least, not directly."

She turned away from him once again, and this time walked the distance of the yard as Elvis raised his head and watched. Lucia stopped at the fence, rested her hands on the top and looked up into the sky. She stood like this for what seemed to be several minutes, before finally turning around. "Adam, tonight you have said things that try my abilities to answer you. Matters that are so simple and obvious to me escape your understanding, and in fact, are far beyond your capabilities." She began to walk across the yard toward Adam once again, and when she reached him, reached out and put a hand on his shoulder.

"Adam, it is not just you. Instead it is all of mankind. You lose sight of one single fact – that God is love. Too much emphasis is placed on things as ridiculous as hopping on one foot while you pray, or turning around three times before entering a sanctuary, or other rules that are manufactured by man."

Adam stared at her. "But that's not an answer. Most any pastor, priest, father, rector, whatever, would argue what you just said."

A simple smile crossed the girl's face. "They would argue with me?"

He laughed. "Well, actually, I doubt most religious people would believe that you're even here. It's too fantastic, too out of the ordinary or even the possible in their eyes. That's why I haven't told anyone – not even Emily."

"Yet, here I stand."

"Indeed. But where does that leave my question?"

Lucia looked away for a moment, and then back at Adam. "The most direct answer that I can give you is that God is love, like I said before."

Adam shook his head. "But that's not an answer to my question."

She turned and began to walk away again. As she did, she said, "Very well; here is your answer. Every religion is completely right." After a few more steps, she added, "And every religion is completely, totally wrong."

After pausing to contemplate her words, Adam said, "Whoa, wait just a second. That's a contradiction, not an answer."

Lucia continued to walk away. "It is an answer, just not one that you can understand. You shouldn't waste questions on things that you cannot possibly comprehend."

"Wait!" Adam called, louder than he intended. "Tomorrow's my last night with you. No, I can't waste a question!"

She stopped and turned around. Flatly and evenly, Lucia said, "Then don't let it be a waste. Remember this: God is love. You cannot possibly imagine how much truth and power are in those three miniscule words." She finally smiled. "Much more important than hopping on one foot or turning in circles." With those words, she turned and walked off into the night.

Elvis had meandered over and sat down beside Adam. He reached down to scratch the dog's head. "Did that make any more sense to you, boy, than it did to me?" He straightened up and looked out into the darkness. "Only one night to go, and I blew tonight on some philosophical nonsense that doesn't affect me one way or the other." After another minute, he turned back to the house. "C'mon Elvis. I'm an idiot."

Behind him, he heard Lucia's voice in the distance. "Perhaps not."

He spun around quickly, but he was alone with the basset hound.

The Twelfth Day

For the second time in a week he navigated the narrow roads of Peaceful Hills cemetery to his parents' graves. Adam was there a little longer this time, and finally left, once again wiping away his tears. As he drove toward the exit, a mound of dirt caught his eye. The deep brown was a stark contrast with the white snow.

Stopping the car, he got out and walked over the frozen ground. A few blackish-green leaves spotted the dirt, the remains of the floral arrangements that had been placed on the grave. There was no headstone yet, only the small aluminum sign placed by the funeral home that read, "Robertson, B."

Adam shook his head. "Aw, Ben, you stupid bastard. Couldn't you have taken care of yourself? Lucia says that you had all kinds of warning signs and just ignored them." He sighed. "Well, you should have done something. Mary needs you. She's still all broken up."

He thought about his wife. "I guess Emily's going to be, too. Maybe they can console each other. Hell, maybe they'll find a couple of guys, and they can even double-date." With the toe of his shoe, Adam reached out and gently kicked the oblong mound of dirt. Slowly he made his way around it, looking at the vision of death before him. "You know, Ben, we sure wasted a lot of time. We were friends in high school, and if it hadn't been for that baseball game, we could've been good friends through the rest of our lives. I know that you were angry, and that you took it out on me, but I have to shoulder my share of the blame as well." He continued pacing in a slow oval. "No, I do. Really. You were mad at me so I gave that anger right back at you, when I could have been reaching out to you. But I blew it; a person can never have too many friends, and I really blew it with you."

He stared at the grave a moment longer. "And hell, I should be mad at you. There you were, getting actual, physical signs that something was wrong, and you just blew them off. Me, I don't have that luxury." Adam shrugged. "Oh, sure, I have a midnight saint telling me that I'm going to die, but there's nothing that I can do about it." He turned toward the small aluminum marker, and yelled at it. "I went to the doctor, Ben! I tried to find out what is going to get me, and I can't! You could have..." his voice faded to a whisper. "...you could have done that."

He fought tears as he stood at the grave, taking deep breaths, clinching and unclinching his fists. "I must be crazy," he finally said. "You know, Ben, talking to you is a lot like talking to God. I seem to be the one making all the noise, and I have no idea if anyone is listening at all."

After a few moments, a voice behind him said, "Someone's always listening, you know."

Adam spun around and saw the groundskeeper that he met a few days ago. "Oh, hello, uh..." he hesitated for a second, "Albert, is it?"

"Yep, Albert. Heard what you said." The man had pulled a pipe and a pouch of tobacco from his pocket, and filled the bowl as he spoke. Putting the stem between his lips, the scruffy man produced a match book, struck fire, and lit the pipe. After a few puffs he continued. "Someone's always listening, like I said. May not seem like it at times, but it's true. Don't you ever forget that." Another puff, and he turned and began walking away.

"But how do I know who was listening?" Adam called after him. "Was it Ben? Was God listening?"

The man kept walking, but finally stopped and shrugged his shoulders. "Well, if no one else, I reckon that I was," he said simply, and continued on.

"Swell," Adam said. He began walking back to the truck. Stopping suddenly, he turned around and looked back as if to say something, but Albert was already gone.

* * * * *

Adam knocked on the door of his daughter's room, and cracked the door open. "Your mother said that you'd already turned in – is everything okay? You didn't even say goodnight."

"I knew that you'd come by – you always tuck me in," Amy's voice came from the darkness. "Besides, I had to go to bed early… it's Christmas Eve!"

He opened the door all the way to let light from the hallway into the room. Walking over to the bed, he straightened the covers around her and then sat down on the bed beside her. "So, in bed so that Santa will know that you're asleep, and bring his sleigh by?"

"Oh, Daddy," she giggled. "But we open presents as soon as we wake up, and if I go to sleep Christmas morning will hurry up and get here."

"And what present are you hoping to open?"

"I want a TechnaPad – I told you that," she answered.

"A TechnaPad?" Adam feigned surprise. "To play games on? That doesn't sound very practical."

"But I can use it at school, and read books, and even draw pictures on it."

"And play games?" he said playfully.

Amy rolled her eyes and gave a big sigh. "Yes, Daddy, I can play games on it."

"Hmmm...I don't know. Sounds like a grown-up present to me. I wouldn't get my hopes up."

The young girl laughed, and turned over. "G'night, Daddy."

He leaned over, kissed the top of her head, and pulled the covers up around her. "Good night."

Adam stood up and turned toward the door, then stopped. He looked back at Amy. "You're growing so very big – more every day. You know, one of these days you'll be going off to college and I won't be able to tell you goodnight. After that you'll start a career, maybe get married, and if you're as lucky as I've been, even start a family of your own." He wiped a tear from his eye. "No, it's precious little time that I have with you, Amy. Do me a favor – when the time comes where I'm not around every night, think about me when you close your eyes and know that I love you. You'll always be my little angel, and I'll always be your dad. Know that no matter how far apart we might be, I will always love you more than anything else in the world. Would you do that for me?"

"I know you'll never leave me, Daddy."

He was thankful that she couldn't see how weak his smile was, or the tears streaming down his face. Adam stepped into the hallway, pulled the door shut, and rested his forehead on the door. "Oh, my little girl..." he whispered softly, "how can I tell you goodbye?"

* * * * *

After pulling himself together, Adam walked into the living room, where Emily was wrapping a present in the floor.

"There you are – I was about to send out a search party. Come help, we just have a few more to go."

He sat down beside her. "I was just having a conversation with Amy about Christmas. I'm glad that we got the TechnaPad – otherwise I'd be in the car trying to find an all-night electronics store."

"Speaking of which," Emily reached over into a large plastic bag and removed a brightly-colored box with the word *TechnaPad* on it. "Want to wrap it?"

"With all my heart." He grabbed a tube of gift paper from a collection of wrapping supplies on the floor, and began the process. "Remember when she was younger, and we had to be Santa's elves, assembling all of the toys? Sometimes we'd be up until two in the morning."

Emily laughed. "And she'd get up at six!"

"Those were the days," Adam said. "You know, the least Santa could have done was to put the toys together himself."

"I guess he was just too busy." They wrapped in silence for a minute, and Emily finally said, "Is everything okay, Adam?"

He shrugged. "Of course – I'm fine. We just have to get these presents wrapped before we can turn in, and personally, I'm enjoying the time with my favorite lady." He kissed her, his lips lingering on hers.

"Nice – and I'd better be your only lady. Now keep wrapping." Handing him another box, she said, "Still, you haven't been yourself lately. In some ways you've been so happy, yet in others, well, it's like you have something massive weighing on your shoulders." She finished wrapping a package, pushed it away, and then looked over at him. "I'm here if you need me, you know."

"Always have been," he said with a smile.

"Always will be," she answered. She scooted over close to him, and rested her chin on his shoulder. "You know, we've only got a couple of packages left. Shall we go on to bed, and finish them in the morning before Amy gets up?"

Adam took her hand. "Tell you what – I want to stay up a little longer, so why don't you go on to bed. I'll wrap the last few and then I'll join you." Kissing her forehead, he added, "I'll put my arms around you and we'll cuddle all night long. Promise."

She stared at him for a full minute, before finally saying, "Okay, but only 'cause I'm tired. And it's under protest – I'd rather have you there with me."

"I'll be there before you know it," he said, and kissed her again.

She stood up, and walked toward the hallway. In the doorway she turned around and said, "I love you, Adam."

"And I love you. Now go get the bed warm for me."

Emily smiled, and disappeared into the hallway.

* * * * *

"So," Adam said into the darkness. He was standing on the edge of the patio, looking across the backyard and beyond into the darkness. As the brilliant flash surged behind him, he felt the warmth of her presence on his skin. "Our final night, Lucia."

"Indeed," the familiar voice said from behind him. "How do you feel about that?" She asked, slowly walking around him.

He hesitated for a moment. "Odd. Sad. Scared."

"How curious. Why?" she said as she faced him.

154

"Odd, Lucia, because I have only one question left that I can ask, and after that this gift that God gave me is over. Sad, because I've enjoyed our conversations," he said with a smile. "You've taught me more than I could ever have imagined one person could know. More than that, you've shown me actual proof that we go on after death. Who in the world wouldn't give anything for that?"

Lucia started at him for a moment, and then said, "But God gives you that proof every day, Adam."

"Yeah, yeah, I know. But it's so easy to question without, well, tangible evidence."

She smiled. "Which is why faith is so important."

"I guess so." He stood there for a moment, not knowing what to say. Finally, he continued. "Well, for whatever time I have left, Lucia, I'm going to miss you."

"It has certainly been my pleasure, Adam," she said, bowing her head to acknowledge his compliment. "I am glad that I was given the opportunity to help you. So why did you say that you were scared?"

"Scared because, well, tonight kind of ends my amnesty." Adam spoke slowly, laboring over every word. "As long as I knew that I'd see you another night, get to ask you another question, I would be alive. But there's always been a certain finality about this night."

"There is, in fact, a finality here," she said softly, her voice comforting him. "I would not expect to see you again on this Earth. But we will meet again, Adam."

Adam stood still for a moment, summoning the courage to ask the question that had been lurking in the back of his mind for days. Tears ran down his cheeks, and he sniffed to clear his running nose. He took a deep breath, almost gulping in air. "How soon?" he asked through the emotion. There was no holding back as he openly sobbed. "How soon, Lucia? Are you taking me now? Am I going to die tomorrow, on Christmas

Day, in front of my family? Should I expect a phone call from the doctor with some horrible news? Is an eighteen-wheeler going to plow into my car on the way to town? Lucia, please, please answer me! When will I die?" he cried loudly, tears streaming down his face, more than a demand than a question.

Lucia sighed, and then walked over to Adam. As she had done before in their discussions, she took his hands in hers. "Adam" she said, "Listen to me carefully."

As before, Adam felt super-charged from her touch. He felt unconditional love, he felt ultimate peace, and he felt total happiness. Adam looked into her eyes, and for a moment, the tears stopped.

"Adam" she continued, "your final question, about your own death..."

"When?" he said weakly.

Lucia sighed. "All your questions, Adam, I have had to try and put into terms that you could understand. God gave me direction and wisdom, but the words were my own. I can only hope that in some way I have aided in God's gift to you. This one question, though, I do have a finite answer for." She looked deeply into his eyes, and grasped his hands tightly. "You ask me on this final night about the exact time of your death. My answer is this, Adam..."

In spite of Lucia and the warmth she exuded, every muscle in Adam's body tensed. His heart was thumping, and even in the cold night air, beads of sweat broke out on his forehead. He took a deep breath, prepared for anything, and whispered, "Tell me – please."

"Very well, then." She paused, and the night seemed to weigh heavy around them. "Adam, I have no idea, no idea at all, when you are going to die."

He pulled slightly back, although she would not release his hands. "Wh-what?" he said, confused. "But on the first night you said–"

"On that first night, my exact words were, *"You, Adam, are going to die.* That is all I said, and all that I was allowed to say that night. It was you and your fear of death that transposed all this onto such an immediate frame of time. I am truly sorry, Adam. But you could not have asked the questions that you asked, nor could you have taken the journey that you did, unless you felt that death was upon you. I did not deceive you. I only allowed you to believe what you wanted to. Which in turn, made you face your fears and doubts, and start dealing with them."

Adam stood transfixed. A sense of relief flooded his body. Had he not been holding onto Lucia, he would have collapsed onto the concrete.

"Make no mistake, Adam," she continued. "I spoke the truth. You are indeed going to die, as did I, as will all mortals. One of the things that was causing you problems with death was that you feared it immensely on one hand, and denied it on the other. Deep down inside you, death was always something in the far, far distance that you thought you would never approach. Make no mistake – it could very well be tomorrow… but it might also be many, many years from now."

"Lucia, I – I…" he stammered, looking for words to express the feelings inside. Adam felt free. He felt alive. "I don't know what to say," he finally choked out.

She smiled. "You don't have to say anything. Just remember every word that has passed between us, for everything that I have told you has been the truth. And never forget that each morning that you wake could very well be your last on this Earth, like it was for your friend Benjamin a few days ago. There might not be a tomorrow. Use that to keep your perspective on the things that are small, and focus on what is truly important to you." She gently released his hands, and then took a step back. "If you stop and think about it, you've accomplished quite a lot in the last twelve days; you've lived

157

your life to its fullest, as if you were about to die. You mended fences that should have been done long ago; you shored up friendships that you had neglected, and you turned your full attention to your family and their future." Lucia smiled. "Imagine if everyone could have the gift that God gave you... how rich everyone's lives would become. Continue to live that way, Adam. Live as if any day could be your last, and you will be the better for it." She stopped and just stood there for a moment, then took a deep breath. "That said, I must ask – where is Elvis? I would like to tell him goodbye – he has been such a pleasure."

Adam looked confused for a moment, and said, "Oh, I... I left him inside because I didn't know, well, what tonight might hold. He wasn't very happy about it... but I can get him."

Lucia shook her head, "Do not bother. While you will not see me here again, I think that perhaps I might be allowed to visit Elvis one last time. I have grown quite attached to him over the last twelve nights." She smiled.

"So God will allow you to come back just to visit a dog?" Adam asked.

"Oh, He's like that," she said with a grin, "He really is." She stepped forward and put her hand over his heart, then whispered, "Get to know Him better, Adam. He's really not some stranger up in the sky. And He loves you so much." She stepped back, took a deep breath, and stared at Adam for a moment. "But for us, Adam, this is our final conversation... on Earth, anyway. To you, my friend, I wish peace and happiness always. I will now take my leave of you. Until we meet again, Adam," she said smiling, then turned and began to simply walk away.

"Lucia!" he said urgently.

As quickly and mysteriously as she had come into his life, Lucia was gone. Adam watched as her figure grew smaller in the distance, starting to skate along the top of the new-fallen snow. He stood transfixed until the tiny dot of light disappeared into the night. He felt completely at peace. Adam heaved a sigh, turned and walked across the patio to the house. He opened the patio door, and Emily fell into his arms.

Tears were streaming down her face as she pressed Adam against her. She kissed his lips, then his face, and then embraced him so tightly that their bodies seemed melded together. "Adam..." she said softly.

"Emily? What the…"

"Shhh", she whispered, silencing his words with a kiss. After a moment, she pulled away enough to look him in the eyes. "Oh Adam. I've been so afraid. From the first time that I saw her."

"Lucia? You saw Lucia?" he asked.

"Saw, and heard. It all made sense. You knew that you were dying. The doctor's exam, the time off, it all fell together," she said tearfully.

"How long have you known?" he asked, astounded that she had been able to keep the knowledge from him.

"I don't know. A few nights. You got out of bed and dressed, and I thought it was so bizarre that I waited for you to go outside, and then watched you through a crack in the curtain. My God, Adam, I couldn't believe what I saw. A ghost – an angel. I didn't know what was happening, but I knew that it wasn't of this world. So I watched. And listened. And when I realized what was happening, I cried a lot – just not so that you could hear."

"Emily, you are so incredibly strong." He pulled her close, burying his head in her shoulder, and started to cry.

Tears flowed from her as well. "Not as strong as you. Now come on – everything's all right. We've got a great life ahead, and there's so much to talk about. But also, it's Christmas… who knows when Amy will get up."

Their embrace grew tighter under the dark, December sky.

Epilogue

Thursday, December 13th, one year later

Adam was not sure exactly what was happening around him, only that some well-orchestrated plan was unfolding while he supposedly slept. Emily had fidgeted nervously all night, raising up to regularly glance over his head, presumably at the clock on Adam's nightstand. At five, she accidentally woke him as she tried to inconspicuously slip out of bed. He had not stirred, however, waiting for her plan to unfold, whatever it might be. For the next hour, he heard the voices of his wife and daughter, sometimes laughing, sometimes giggling, as they hatched their mysterious scheme.

A little before six, he heard the bedroom door open, and the room filled with light. He sat up in bed, and saw his daughter Amy parading into the room, carrying a tray that contained a coffee carafe and a plate of pastries. She was dressed in a white robe with a bright red sash tied around her waist, and on her head was a crown of seven candles, each with a candle-flame bulb at the top. Greenery was woven around the crown, a beautiful contrast to the child's red hair. As she

161

entered, Amy sang, "Si-lent Night... Ho-ly Night... All is calm... All is bright..."

Emily came in behind her in her house-robe, and then climbed in bed beside Adam. She helped her daughter lift the tray onto the bed, and then Amy jumped onto the foot, upsetting her crown. Elvis trotted into the room, and plopped down on the carpet.

"Happy Saint Lucia's Day, daddy!" the young girl said, her smile beaming brighter than the candles.

Adam looked at his wife suspiciously. "Okay, so what gives?"

"Amy said it best... Happy Saint Lucia's Day." She reached over and kissed Adam. "It's a tradition in the Scandinavian countries – in the early morning of the day, the eldest daughter portrays Saint Lucia, with a crown of candles on her head." She leaned over and whispered "Battery powered, in our case, for safety." Winking and sitting back up, Emily continued. "Coffee and Lucia buns, which are special pastries, are served to the parents in bed, while the kids sing Lucia carols."

Amy laughed. "Mom said that apple turnovers from the grocery store would be fine, and since I didn't know any of the Lucia songs, *Silent Night* would probably work."

"I think that this is the most special morning that I've had in a long time," Adam said proudly, and bit into one of the pastries.

For the next half-hour, the trio sat on the bed, in the light provided by the Lucia crown, and talked about the upcoming Christmas holidays, shopping, presents, all the food that would be prepared, and everything magical about the season.

Emily finally glanced over at the clock. "Oh, wow, we've got to get ready. Amy, you're going to be late for school if you don't get going, and your dad and I have to hustle to get dressed for work."

Amy kissed them both, and then ran out of the room, both hands clutching her Lucia crown to keep it from falling. Elvis ran after her at a trot.

Emily and Adam stood up on their respective sides, stretched, met at the foot of the bed for a kiss, and then went about the business of their morning dressing rituals.

Adam paused at the window as he walked by, pulling the curtain aside, and staring into the darkness that was just beginning to be pierced by the rays of the rising sun. His wife walked over, put her head on his shoulder, and looked out as well.

"You hoping to see her again?" she asked.

He laughed, "Well, it is Saint Lucia's Day, and it's certainly not a common thing to talk with an actual saint." After a minute, he added, "Besides, I've thought of a few dozen additional questions that I'd like to ask her."

It was Emily's turn to chuckle. "Well, based on what she said on that last night, I hope it's a very long time until you get to ask her anything again."

"Amen." He closed the curtain, and walked into their dressing room.

As Emily followed and went to the closet, she stopped and said, "Do you think that you'll ever tell Amy about your evenings with Lucia?"

He squirted shaving cream into his hand, and then began to rub it onto his face. "One of these days. If I did it now, though, she'd tell her friends, they'd tell their parents, and before long everyone in town would think that I was crazy. Someday, though."

As she passed by, Emily casually said, "I wonder what Lucia would say about that..." and then continued on to the bathroom.

Adam started to shave, and then stopped suddenly. Looking into his own eyes in the mirror, he said, "She'd probably point out that it's always possible that someday might never come."

* * * * *

As he drove to work, Adam could not stop thinking about Emily's words that morning, and Lucia's a year ago.

Annabel, the office admin, spoke as Adam came through the door. "Well, good morning – are you counting the days until Christmas?"

"That I am, Ms. Neeves, that I am." Adam walked past the front desk, and then stopped. "Oh, I almost forgot to mention... I have an extremely important project that has to be finished as soon as possible, so if you can help hide me, I'd really appreciate it."

"Got it – you're in a meeting as far as anyone else is concerned," Annabel said with a wink and a smile.

"Great. Much appreciated." Adam walked down the hall to his office, closed the door as he went inside, and then sat down at his desk. He ignored his email, closed the daily pop-up calendar on the screen, and went straight to his word processor. Taking a deep breath, and breathing it out slowly, he proceeded to type the story...

> "How far?"
> "About a hundred-thirty miles, or seventeen gallons of gas, based on the last tank," she said, staring at the map and mentally adding the numbers between the state line and Little Rock. "Wait, we're still thirty miles from the state line so add another couple of gallons."
> "Crap," Daniel sighed under his breath, closing his eyes and resting his face in his hands. "We're in some real trouble here, Jen..."

When Adam finally took a break, several hours had passed. He saved the file, stood up and stretched, and then walked out into the hallway. It was going to be a good day. It was going to be a good life.